SARA'S LATEST SCHEME

Uncle Alec continued silently scanning the article, unmindful that Sara's attention had suddenly fixed on the paper, too. She peered over Uncle Alec's shoulder at the accompanying photograph.

"He's handsome. Is he rich?"

Her voice remained neutral but her eyes were already gleaming.

"Whew, sure is. Made a fortune in pulp and paper."

"But that's it!" cried Sara. "Someone who's rich. That's who we should ask for a donation."

Aunt Janet burst into laughter. "They say since Wellington Campbell made his money he's as hard to talk to as the King of England."

If Aunt Janet thought this would discourage Sara, she had another thing coming.

"Where is he staying?" she wanted to know.

"Uh, the White Sands Hotel."

Sara smiled. After all, if you want to catch a tiger, the first thing you do is track him to his lair. . . .

The Story Girl Earns Her Name

Storybook written by

Gail Hamilton

Based on the Sullivan Films Production
written by Heather Conkie
adapted from the novels of

Lucy Maud Montgomery

A BANTAM SKYLARK BOOK
NEW YORK · TORONTO · LONDON · SYDNEY · AUCKLAND

Based on the Sullivan Films Production produced by Sullivan Films Inc.
in association with CBC and the Disney Channel with the participation
of Telefilm Canada adapted from Lucy Maud Montgomery's novels.
Teleplay written by Heather Conkie. Copyright © 1989 by Sullivan
Films Distribution, Inc.

This edition contains the complete text
of the original edition.
NOT ONE WORD HAS BEEN OMITTED.

RL 6, 008–012

THE STORY GIRL EARNS HER NAME

A Bantam Skylark Book / published by arrangement with
HarperCollins Publishers Ltd.

PRINTING HISTORY
HarperCollins edition published 1991
Bantam edition / June 1992
ROAD TO AVONLEA is the trademark of Sullivan Films Inc.

Skylark Books is a registered trademark of Bantam Books,
a division of Bantam Doubleday Dell Publishing Group, Inc.
Registered in U.S. Patent and Trademark Office and elsewhere.

ISBN 0-553-48028-6
UK ISBN 0-553-40576-4

PRINTED IN THE UNITED STATES OF AMERICA

OPM   0 9 8 7 6 5 4

The Story Girl Earns Her Name

Chapter One

"I can't believe it," Felix King exclaimed. "There's going to be a real magic lantern show, right here in Avonlea!"

He said this over a great mouthful of hard candy, which he was munching on the steps of the Avonlea general store. In company with his sisters, Felicity and Cecily, and his cousins, Sara Stanley and Andrew King, he was ogling the bulletin board, which announced all public events of importance in Avonlea. Today it had a single poster spread grandly across its middle. BEATTY'S MAGIC LANTERN SHOW, the poster announced, to be held at the Avonlea Town Hall that very evening. "Sold Out!" was stamped in huge letters across the announcement. All the proceeds were to go to the Avonlea School library.

Felicity King inspected the bold print as though to make sure the momentous event was really going to take place. Avonlea was a quiet village, and entertainment spectacles of this magnitude were rare indeed.

"I'm looking forward to it so much. Mother said I could wear my best pink muslin."

Felicity was Felix's older sister and would never dream of speaking with her mouth full. Felicity was tidy, practical and very particular about her own dignity. Her eyes were already alight with a vision of herself swishing up the Town Hall steps in her best, most becoming dress. Cecily, Felix's younger sister, was too small to care about how she looked. She stopped sucking on her candy altogether, imagining the wonders of the show itself.

"I can't wait! I've never seen a magic lantern show before!"

"I've seen lots of them," put in Sara Stanley. "In Montreal, father used to take me all the time!"

"Well, la-de-da!" was Felicity's answer to that, lest Sara give herself airs about her fancy upbringing.

Sara had grown up in Montreal, with her own

nanny and more muslin dresses than any one girl could possibly need. But all that was before her father's financial troubles had sent her to stay with her Aunts Hetty and Olivia in Avonlea. Sara hadn't been in Avonlea very long, and she was having all the usual troubles trying to fit herself into the tightly knit rural community. The other children, especially, weren't sure whether or not they liked this dreamy, city-bred cousin from "away." "Away" was what Prince Edward Islanders called any place outside their sea-bound province.

Felicity was having the hardest time adjusting to Sara. Up until Sara came, Felicity, the eldest girl among the King children, had been able to queen it over the rest. Now Sara, at twelve almost as old as Felicity, was challenging her leadership.

Felix was much more interested in the magic lantern itself. Magic lanterns had been the rage for as long as he could remember, and he was dying to get his hands on one.

"Maybe the fellow will let us see how it works."

"It's really pretty simple."

So said Andrew King. Andrew was staying with Aunt Janet and Uncle Alec King while his father, Uncle Alec's brother, Alan, was in South America working as a geologist. Andrew was good with his hands and prided himself on knowing lots and lots of useful things.

"Oh, good, then there's half a chance even Felix might understand!"

Felicity tossed off this sarcasm as she took another nibble of her candy and went back to playing jacks with Cecily. They were all waiting for Aunt Olivia, who was inside the store.

"And no chance you will, Felicity!" Felix shot back. It was a point of honor with Felix not to be downtrodden by his sister, even though his resistance didn't often succeed.

"See," Andrew explained, drawing diagrams in the air with his hands, "they've got these glass slides with pictures painted on them, and they put the slides between the lens and a light source, and then project them onto the screen.... Understand?"

Whether he did or not, Felix nodded vigorously. Andrew's explanations got more technical. Sara approached the game of jacks, but Felicity's back was firmly turned. With a sigh, Sara stepped away again. Since there seemed nothing for it but to amuse herself, Sara began to stroll beyond the store a little bit, savouring her peppermint stick.

It was still very early in the morning, and that added a special pleasure to the candy. Dew sparkled on the grass and breakfast smells wafted onto Avonlea's single street. No matter how many magic lantern shows she had seen, Sara still got excited about them. She, too, looked forward to the one tonight, hoping it wouldn't be just nice, instructive travel slides, but a gripping story. Sara had an imagination—rather more imagination than was good for her, her Aunt Hetty thought—and loved stories, the more dramatic and heart-rending the better. Tales about ghosts or shipwrecks sent chills right up her spine, even if they had happy endings. Star-crossed lovers parted by cruel circumstance were thrilling too. Or maybe...

A sharp thud above Sara's head startled her out of her daydreams. She looked up. Could that be a valise emerging from that upstairs window? And a man's leg struggling to get out behind it?

It was indeed. And at the Avonlea boarding house too.

The sight was so extraordinary that Sara simply stood there, open-mouthed, as the rest of the man tried to follow the leg and ended up stuck halfway over the windowsill. When the man got his head out, the first thing he saw was Sara, leaning over the picket fence, staring up at him. He was a beefy, ruddy gent, but he turned rather pale at finding himself observed and squeezed out a hurried laugh. With the hand that wasn't clutching the valise, he pointed down toward the door.

"Oh, heh, heh, that door sticks all the time. Have to use the window."

Sara herself had had to climb out the odd window in her time, and she knew it to be a very uncomfortable practice.

"You could hurt yourself," she told him, finding her tongue at last. "Someone should fix that. Would you like me to get someone?"

"Oh—no, no thanks!"

The idea of bothering someone at that early hour to fix a door seemed to fluster the fellow so that he banged his head on the window sash in a renewed attempt to get the rest of himself through. From inside, a woman's voice floated out.

"Mr. Beatty, your breakfast is ready."

Breakfast must have been an alarming idea, for the man jerked himself all the way out onto the porch roof and looked wildly about. His gaze lit upon a horse and buggy tied up in front of the general store. Gingerly, he edged down toward the eaves and motioned to Sara.

"Ah...there is something you could do for me. Bring my horse and carriage over so I can jump into it, would you?"

"Mr. Beatty, Mr Beatty," sang out the voice from inside again. "Are you there?"

The man now had one leg hanging down over

the roof edge and looked as though he wanted his horse and buggy very urgently indeed. It never occurred to Sara to hesitate. She had already untied the horse and was starting to lead it toward the boarding house when Andrew spotted her.

"Hey," he shouted, "what do you think you're doing?"

"Just helping someone out."

Sara was helpful by nature, and especially pleased when she could help someone out of a fix. The man, by this time, had taken a daring leap from the roof edge straight down into the petunia bed.

"But isn't that Mr. Biggins' buggy?"

Felicity had now spied Sara and jumped up right in the middle of a game of jacks.

"No it isn't," Sara tossed back. It was ridiculous that the man wouldn't know his own rig.

"It is so Mr. Biggins' buggy," Felicity sputtered, starting after her cousin. "I saw him go into the store."

Felicity was too late. The man had already cleared the yard fence, flung his valise into the back of the buggy and jumped up into the driver's seat.

"Thank you, miss," he said to Sara, snatching up the reins and grinning a sly, triumphant grin.

With a great thwack, he laid the whip across the horse's back, sending the surprised beast leaping down the street, the buggy careening behind it. Dust choked Sara at exactly the same moment Mr. Biggins and Mr. Lawson tore out of the store to see what all the commotion was about. Mr. Biggins saw what was the matter at once.

"Stop!" he shrieked. "That's my buggy!"

Dropping the bag of flour he was carrying, Mr. Biggins began to run after the speeding vehicle. The bag of flour burst on the ground behind him, spilling flour everywhere. Mr. Lawson, the storekeeper, who had just sold Mr. Biggins that flour, barely noticed. He had just recognized the buggy's driver.

"Why, that man owes me fifty dollars in merchandise. Come back!"

Mr. Lawson waved his arms in futile fury, bringing his wife and Olivia King running out onto the store steps. Mr. Biggins, still shouting, "Come back with my horse!" was puffing along as fast as his legs would carry him. He was no match for the horse, but his shouts did reach Constable Jeffries, who was standing in front of the blacksmith's shop, thumbs tucked into his suspenders. Constable Jeffries started blowing his whistle frantically as the buggy jolted by.

"Stop, in the name of the law!"

All he got for his trouble was a mouthful of road dirt and a split second to jump for his life. He landed in the smith's pile of hay, luckier by far than the two ladies farther down the road. They ended up upside down in the ditch in the wake of the galloping rig.

Mr. Biggins wheezed up, his feet dragging to a halt. "Stop...thief," he managed one last time, the words barely a gasp. Mr. Biggins was purple with rage; he was much too old and too fat to be chasing stolen buggies through the street at eight o'clock in the morning.

All the shouts in Avonlea wouldn't have done any good. The buggy skidded round the bend at the far end of the road, nearly running over a cyclist for good measure, then vanished completely from sight.

Back in front of the store, all was upset and confusion.

"Why, that was Mr. Beatty," declared Olivia King as though scarcely able to credit her own eyesight.

Felicity glared at Sara, who was still frozen rigid by what had just happened. "I told you it was Mr. Biggins' buggy," Felicity hissed. Righteous indignation was Felicity's specialty.

"He ran up quite a bill at our store," Mrs. Lawson contributed. "I told my husband not to trust him."

Olivia scarcely heard this. Her hand suddenly flew to her mouth. This was the same Mr. Beatty mentioned so prominently on the nearby poster.

"Oh, my goodness. What about the magic lantern show?"

Prospects of the evening's entertainment disappeared before Olivia's very eyes. Olivia had an optimistic nature, however, and instantly discovered something positive to pull from the mess.

"Oh, well, it's a good thing the ticket money is safe with you, Mr. Lawson."

This simple statement produced astonishment in the storekeeper. "But Mr. Beatty said you had the proceeds, Olivia!"

"Why would I have the proceeds! He said you had them...."

As the awful realization dawned, silence struck them all.

"Oh no!" breathed Olivia when she'd recovered herself. The money, so painstakingly collected, was even then heading for parts unknown in Mr. Beatty's valise.

Mr. Biggins came lurching back. He had had time to brood on the wrong done him and was working himself into a fine old lather. Horses and buggies weren't easy to come by. Neither were bags of flour.

"I'd like to know how that man got hold of my horse and buggy!" Mr. Biggins rapped out, looking as though he would like to make chopped mincemeat out of the culprit right then and there.

Felicity pointed sweepingly at Sara.

"*She* gave it to him!"

Every eye turned and fixed itself on Sara, who had red dust in her hair and dismay written all over her.

"Oh, Sara," cried Olivia, "how could you?"

"I didn't know it wasn't his buggy!"

This might have been perfectly true, but in the eyes of the gathered group, it seemed a sorry excuse for the calamity that had fallen upon them. It's all my fault, Sara thought miserably, knowing that guilt had just begun to haunt her. Now all of Avonlea would make up its mind that it detested her.

And Felicity! If Sara stayed in Avonlea a hundred years, Felicity would never let her hear the end of this!!

Chapter Two

News of the disaster spread over Avonlea with the speed of lightning. Naturally, it arrived in Olivia's own kitchen even before she and Sara had made their way back from the store. When they got home, they had to deal with Aunt Hetty, Olivia's older sister and the straitlaced head of the household.

In fact, Hetty was more than head of the household. As the eldest of the King brothers and sisters, she regarded herself as head of the King clan in particular and arbiter of morals in Avonlea in general. She came by this last role quite honestly. Aunt Hetty was the Avonlea schoolmistress. She had probably hammered more edifying precepts into more reluctant little heads than anyone else for fifty miles around. She and Olivia, being both unmarried, lived together in Rose Cottage. Things ran smoothly so long as Olivia deferred to whatever Hetty said.

Olivia took off her hat and set about making a soothing cup of tea. She used the pretty teapot, with the violets on it, and cut slices of pound cake as thin as Hetty liked. Sara went straight to a corner and sat down, head bowed in ignominy, unable to utter a word.

"Mr. Beatty seemed like such a nice, honest man," Olivia protested when she and Hetty finally sat down to tea. "He gave me his word."

The pound cake failed to mollify Aunt Hetty. Her brows shot up in her best "I-told-you-so" manner. Hetty had a great fondness for getting in the last word.

"Men who run travelling shows are seldom known for their honor, Olivia. This is a fine kettle of fish. I can't think why I let you talk me into dealing with that ridiculous man and his back street sideshow."

"But Hetty..."

Olivia remembered just how much persuasion it had taken. Yet since Hetty had finally agreed, it didn't seem fair for her to be pointing a finger now.

"Magic lantern indeed!" Hetty snorted, still ignoring the pound cake.

Olivia stole a glance at Sara and tried another tack. Olivia had the kindest of hearts and couldn't bear to see Sara drooping so.

"It was a very popular idea," she ventured. "All the tickets were sold and—"

"And!" Hetty shook off Olivia's meek effort and fixed her attention on the other occupant of the room. "As for you, Sara Stanley, when will you ever learn to look before you leap? You and Olivia, cut from the same cloth. You're too...trusting. Sometimes I wonder if either of you has the sense that God gave you."

Satisfied that she'd delivered a just rebuke, Hetty finished her tea in silence and then sailed from the room. Ever since Sara's arrival in Avonlea, nanny in tow, Hetty had regarded the girl as a scandalously indulged creature who needed a firm hand to whip her into shape. After packing off the nanny, Hetty had undertaken the job. Since then, Sara and Hetty had had a number of struggles that only served to confirm Hetty's opinion. Now Olivia was included in the blame, simply because she had been enthusiastic about a magic lantern show. Hetty left Sara and Olivia staring glumly at each other, their hearts heavy and their supply of sense from the good Lord deeply in doubt.

The exit of Mr. Beatty with the ticket proceeds left unanswered the purpose for the show in the first place—to raise money for the school library. As guardian of culture in the village, Aunt Hetty meant to have more books, and she was not likely to be daunted by one setback. A woman of strong will and unbending principle, she had never approved of the magic lantern show. It had smacked too much of easy pleasure. Now, with the failure of Olivia's newfangled idea, Hetty returned to her old standby—plain hard work for a good cause. At the end of the next school day, she rapped her pointer sharply on her desk and addressed the roomful of children.

"As I'm sure you all know by now, the effort to raise money for the school library by joining forces with Mr. Beatty has proven unsuccessful."

She paused, as she always did before launching into a juicy moral. In the interval, everyone, including Aunt Hetty, stared at a very long-faced Sara.

"Bad beginnings need not make bad endings," Hetty continued, just a little self-satisfied. "And we must now follow through with my original plan. I want each of you to try to raise money on your own for the project."

"Here comes the part about 'honest toil,'" Felix whispered to Andrew.

"Raise money," Hetty went on, "with the rewards of honest toil, or by gathering contributions from friends and family. Now, make sure you explain just what it is they are contributing to and of what value it is. Class dismissed."

Released, the Avonlea children erupted from the schoolhouse door and started in their several directions home. Many had a long walk ahead of them and chores waiting when they got there. Sara, looking very despondent, came down the steps with Felicity and Cecily. Clemmie Ray, Cecily's friend, tagged along behind.

"We just have to think of a way to make some money," Sara said, remorse over the loss of the library funds weighing on her like a millstone. "I feel completely responsible for the failure of the magic lantern show."

"You *are* completely responsible," declared Felicity. She could have said more, but just then she was almost knocked over by Edward Ray, who was running past at top speed. Edward was a rough boy, with hair sticking out like bits of straw and big, thumping boots.

"Better hurry home, Clemmie," he called to his sister. "Before Ma gives you a licking."

Mrs. Ray was fearsome for her strictness, but Clemmie bravely stuck with her friends. Others, who weren't friends, sidled over and gave Clemmie the fishy eye.

"I suppose we can't expect too much from you, can we, Clemmie?" Sally Potts said.

Clemmie shook her head stoutly. "My mother won't give me a cent. She thinks books build a pathway to the devil."

"My rich uncle is visiting from Charlottetown," Sally crowed, her nose high in the air. "He will be glad to donate to the cause. I'm bound to raise the most money."

This was Sally's way of making fun of Sara, and it stung, as it was meant to. Any new child in a new school has to struggle to get accepted. One such as Sara, who had real lace on her collars, dainty manners and Felicity King for a cousin, was made to undergo tortures. Sally Potts, nasty and moon-faced, led the faction against her. Sally envied everything Sara stood for, but made no effort to foster similar improvements in herself.

Sara didn't suffer meekly, though. Even though she was wrapped up in her own troubles, she made a horrid face at Sally behind her back. Sally seemed to sense it through the back of her head because she suddenly swung round. "Wherever did you get that dress, Sara?"

"My father sent it to me. It's from Paris."

Sara was merely stating a fact, but in Avonlea no one had dresses from Paris. To say so meant one was unbearably stuck-up. Sally rolled her eyes at Jane, her companion in mischief.

"Oh, Jane, isn't that too exciting! Do you think I could borrow it some time, Sara?"

"If you think it would fit you."

Sara looked pointedly at Sally's fat stomach. Sally laughed sneeringly.

"I wasn't going to wear it. It will make a good rag to wash the floor with."

This was too much for Felicity. Kings stood up for their own, no matter how much they fought among themselves. Besides, she knew lots of things about Avonlea that Sara didn't, and she could use them to telling effect.

"I wouldn't give myself such airs, Sally Potts! Your kitchen doesn't even have a real floor, just hard-pressed dirt!"

The shot struck its target. Sally and Jane, as one, stuck out their tongues and marched haughtily away. Sally was good at attacking other people, but not at taking spirited retaliation in return.

"Don't pay any attention to them, Sara," Cecily piped up. She admired her cousin from Montreal enormously and wanted to do her best to protect her.

"I don't intend to," answered Sara, still distracted by the greater problem weighing on her. "There are far more important things to think about. We have to figure out how to make the most money for the library. More than Miss Frog-faced Sally Potts."

The idea of beating Sally Potts seemed to be just the spur Sara needed. Brightening, she began to get that determined look she got when she meant to accomplish a thing, no matter what the cost. If she could just bring in enough money for the library fund to make up for the magic lantern show, her conscience would stop torturing her. She'd no longer feel like a criminal every time she walked down the street in Avonlea.

Clemmie had her own solution.

"I'm just going to pray to God to send me some money."

"That won't do any good," Felix told her. Felix already had a lot of experience praying for things he never got. At various times he had begged for bicycles, train sets and better marks in spelling, none of which had yet materialized.

Felicity, who knew a lot more about how divine Providence worked, tossed him a scornful look.

"God gives lots of things, but He doesn't give money. People can earn that for themselves."

"I can't," Clemmie pointed out reasonably. "I think He should take that into account."

Discounting God, Felix turned to earthly possibilities.

"I bet our relatives are good for a dollar each, anyway."

This added up to an impressive sum. Felicity immediately latched onto the idea.

"Father will give us more than that. You'll see."

Both Felix and Felicity had overestimated badly, as they discovered at home that evening. Sara was with them as their father drew out his pocketbook, extracted five quarters and laid them in a row on the kitchen table.

"There, a quarter each to get you started. How's that?"

Uncle Alec was so pleased at his own generosity that it took him several moments to realize that joy and gratitude weren't exactly shining from the five young faces around the table.

"Well, what's wrong?" he demanded.

"Nothing's wrong, Uncle Alec," Sara began. It's just—"

She broke off, loath to admit what high hopes she, too, had entertained of the King family grown-ups.

"Oh, you were expecting more, were you?" Uncle Alec pulled the corners of his mouth down ironically. "Well, I'm afraid that's going to have to do. If you want more, you'll have to earn it yourselves."

Uncle Alec, like Aunt Hetty, had his own ideas about what built character in young people. Felicity, to her credit, attempted to rise to the occasion. "I could have a bake sale and, Felix, you could do some weeding."

"I don't like weeding," cried Felix, alarmed at the possibility. Felicity made awfully free with other people's labor and he meant to avoid being entrapped if at all possible.

Felicity wrinkled her nose. "Lazy boys never do. They have to bend down too much."

Sara sighed. "The bake sale and weeding will never earn enough."

"Fine, then," snapped Felicity. "You come up with something better if you're so smart."

The one thing Sara was never short of was ideas. In a wink, she accepted Felicity's challenge.

"All right, we will canvass every house in Avonlea. People are bound to contribute to such a worthy cause."

Sara had a personal interest in the school library. Books were, to her, like drink to a traveller in the desert. Even in the short time she had been in Avonlea, Sara had read most of the books on the library shelves. If the school didn't get some additions soon, Sara would be forced to start the second time round.

"I will not go begging from door to door," Felicity declared. She went to help her mother with dinner, fiercely jabbing the masher into a pot of boiled potatoes.

Sara smiled to herself. Felicity was proud, but Sara Stanley knew just how to get round that.

"Would you rather Miss Sally Potts contribute more than the Kings, Felicity?"

It was the spectre of a triumphant Sally that finally did the trick. Grumbling, Felicity went with the rest of the children the next day to canvass the houses of Avonlea—not that it did the library fund very much good. After the last house had been tramped to, the canvassers flopped down wearily around the King kitchen table and counted the take.

"Two dollars and fifteen cents."

Andrew laid the coins out side by side, but they wouldn't have covered a pixie's handkerchief.

"That's all?" Felix croaked. He felt he had hiked his boot soles through in pursuit of that money.

"Plus the quarters I gave you," Uncle Alec, sitting in the corner with the newspaper, reminded them.

"Three dollars and forty cents," Andrew amended glumly.

"It won't buy many books," Sara sighed. In fact, it wouldn't keep her in reading material for more than a week or two.

Felicity, still smarting from the humiliations she had had to endure on Avonlea doorsteps, looked scornfully at the money.

"'People are bound to contribute to such a worthy cause,'" she mimicked, in a deadly imitation of Sara's inspiring speech. "Some contributions! I still haven't got the goose feathers out of my hair!"

The people of Avonlea were sober, hard-working folk. At best, they regarded reading as a luxury only for the idle. At worst, like Clemmie's mother, they thought it a direct path to sloth and ruin. Either way, they certainly weren't about give their money away to children who should have had better things to do than go round asking for it.

Cries of "Tomfoolery!" "Nonsense!" and "Ridiculous charity!" had driven the little troop of collectors away from door after door empty-handed. The worst had been when Sara and Felicity accidentally left Mrs. Simpson's gate open so that her flock of geese got out all over the road. As anyone who has ever tried to catch a determined goose can tell you, Sara and Felicity didn't finish that episode until they were scratched up, muddied all over and exhausted from the chase.

Keeping his opinion to himself, Uncle Alec kept on reading the paper. He made it calmly through the political news, church announcements and farm implements for sale. But when he got to the social section, he stopped short.

"Will you look at this, Janet," he said to his wife. "It says here that Wellington Campbell has returned to his home town of Avonlea to look for a property. Remember him?"

Aunt Janet paused in her crocheting.

"Yes. Well, I remember what he was like

before he got all high and mighty."

"Seems to me he wants a place on the Island to get away from it all."

Uncle Alec continued silently scanning the article, unmindful that Sara's attention had suddenly fixed on the paper, too. Slowly she rose from her chair and peered over Uncle Alec's shoulder at the accompanying photograph.

"He's handsome. Is he rich?"

Her voice remained neutral but her eyes were already gleaming. Not that Uncle Alec noticed. He was usually the last to find out when Sara Stanley had a new idea hatching. He grinned at her question.

"Whew, sure is. Made a fortune in pulp and paper."

"Off the sweat of other men's backs," Aunt Janet added tartly, giving her crochet thread a jerk. She thought people should do their own sweating if they meant to get rich.

"But that's it!" cried Sara, seeing only a well-stuffed wallet. "Someone who's rich. That's who we should ask for a donation."

Aunt Janet burst into laughter. "They say since Wellington Campbell made his money he's as hard to talk to as the King of England."

If Aunt Janet thought this would discourage Sara, she had another think coming. Sara now felt doubly responsible—for the failure of the magic lantern show *and* the canvassing effort—and she had to make it up somehow. When her jaw took the set it did at that moment, even the King of England didn't seem safe from her.

"Where is he staying?" she wanted to know. Uncle Alec ran his finger all the way to the bottom of the article.

"Uh, the White Sands Hotel."

Sara smiled. After all, if you want to catch a tiger, the first thing you do is track him to his lair.

Chapter Three

The White Sands Hotel was one of Prince Edward Island's most imposing establishments, sitting majestically in the midst of manicured lawns overlooking the sea. It was well named, too, because of the wide, sparkling white beaches stretching to the water. Turrets rose from its roof, pillars guarded its doors, waiters in smart white coats served tea on the broad, flowery terraces. Even the shingles on its gables were ornate. Wealthy tourists came here from every place imaginable to admire the coastline's sweeping beauty and stuff themselves with the superb seafood that was the hotel's specialty.

Facing this magnificence was a brave band of children: Andrew, Felix, Felicity, Cecily and Peter Craig, the hired hand at the King Farm—all led by Sara.

Felix had never really been close to the White Sands before and he was rapidly losing his nerve. All of them in fact, apart from Sara, looked decidedly less resolute than they had ten minutes earlier.

"We can't go in there," Felix croaked, biting his lip. Up until then, he had thought the Avonlea Town Hall the very height of architectural grandeur.

"Nonsense," replied Sara confidently. "I've been in much grander hotels than the White Sands."

She managed to rally her party enough to get them up the wide front steps and into the lobby of the hotel. Here, she lost just a little of her assurance. It was true she had been in much grander hotels than this, but she had been in them with her father. Her father, in his elegant tailcoat and his silk cravat, had belonged there; the children with Sara didn't. They stood out like sore thumbs among the oriental carpets, marble carvings and settees covered in luxurious red velvet.

On top of this, a formidable man was standing by the desk chatting to a couple ruddy from a walk by the sea. With his beady eye and air of command, he was probably the manager. Sara knew very well that managers could eat alive anyone who was not a paying guest.

Beside her, Felix was looking alarmingly queasy. "Maybe we should give up and go home. This is only for rich people."

Well, rich people were just what they wanted. Sara saw she had to deal firmly with Felix.

"You can go home if you like, but I'm going to see Mr. Campbell. I warn you, though, if he gives me anything, I'll keep it all for my own donation."

This threat didn't have much of an effect on Felix. He was paralyzed by the sight of the manager bearing down on them. The manager made shooing motions, as if the children were so many farm chickens who had got in at the door by mistake.

"Off you go now. We don't want any of you children annoying the guests."

Sara was not about to be shooed out like a stray hen. She drew herself up to her full height— approximately up to the manager's third shirt button—and looked the man straight in the eye.

"We weren't annoying anyone!"

For just a moment, her imperious tone took the manager aback, and he stopped his shooing motion. Before he had a chance to start again, a handsomely dressed pair glided through the door across from him. The man was tall and vigorous, with thick black hair and a waxed, handlebar mustache. The woman smiled continually up at him and wore enough striped damask to upholster half a dozen couches. They must have been important, because the manager dashed right over to them.

"Ah, Mr. Campbell—and Mrs. Tarbush! How very good to see you. Will be joining us for lunch?"

The manager wasn't shooing these people. He was bowing obsequiously.

"We will," said Mr. Campbell, taking the lady's arm. Mrs. Tarbush beamed even more glowingly as they followed the manager through the tall French doors into the adjoining dining room. The children took the opportunity to scurry across the lobby to the wall nearest the dining-room entrance.

"It's him! He looks exactly like his picture." Sara whispered excitedly. She hadn't guessed it would be so easy to find the object of her search.

Felicity stuck her head next to Sara's, almost bumping foreheads. They were both trying to see, while doing their best to keep a large potted palm between themselves and the manager.

"And he's with the widow Tarbush," Felicity

contributed. "Aunt Hetty can't stand her. She's always coming over and borrowing eggs and never ever pays for them."

They watched the manager seat the two at a table gleaming with crystal and heavy silverware.

"May I?" He pushed Mrs. Tarbush's chair in with a flourish and bowed again to Mr. Campbell. It was amazing the miracles that money could inspire.

"I believe we have one of your favourite dishes on the menu today, sir. Lobster bisque."

When she saw the manager leaving the table, Sara knew she had to move fast. Swiftly, she looked around, then grabbed the unfortunate Felix.

"Come on. I have an idea!"

Felix certainly didn't want to know what it was, but he was dragged around the corner anyway. "Sara, Felix, where are you going?" Felicity called in a loud whisper, following after nevertheless. They were now in the vast dining room, and Felicity knew for sure they shouldn't be there. The manager was just leaving, and he pounced on Andrew, Cecily and Peter, who hadn't been fast enough to follow Sara. They could hardly keep from shaking under his wrath.

"I thought I told you children to get out of here. Out!"

Before the three knew what had happened, they were being whisked bodily through the busy lobby and practically flung outside on the steps. The experience so frightened them that they took to their heels as fast as they could, leaving Sara, Felicity and Felix to whatever awful fate they might meet back in the hotel.

Inside, Sara left her safe corner and began a purposeful march across the dining room. Felicity, much impeded by Felix hanging tightly onto her arm, hissed urgently for Sara to come back. When Sara ignored her, Felicity shook her brother loose and set out after her. Sara might be crazy, but Felicity wasn't going to let her reap the benefits of it all on her own.

"I'm not going to let her get away with keeping all the money for herself," she muttered. "Come on, Felix."

The two scuttled from palm tree to palm tree, trying to catch up. They had almost made it when, right before Felicity's horrified gaze, Sara dropped from sight. Or rather, dropped to her knees and crawled under a vacant dining table, hiding completely under the heavy linen cloth.

Felicity stopped in her tracks, ready to demand furiously just what Sara thought she was doing. Then she, too, caught sight of the maitre d', not ten yards away, discussing the menu with some silk-clad guests. In a flash, Felicity and Felix had dropped under the table, too. In any fancy dining room, the maitre d' is the ruler. If anything, this man was even scarier than the manager outside.

Felix was crammed against a table leg so tightly he didn't even have room to shake in his shoes.

"Sara, we're going to get caught!" Felicity hissed through gritted teeth, wondering if Andrew, Peter and Cecily had already been arrested and carted off to jail.

"Shhh," warned Sara, struggling hard to avoid being pushed out onto the open floor. "There isn't enough room. Be quiet or he'll hear!"

Out of the corner of his eye, the maitre d' caught sight of the table doing a little dance all on its own. Since tables didn't dare dance in *his* dining room, he refused to believe his own senses. When he looked again, the table stood still, and he was too far away to see the bulges in the cloth that were Sara's knees. Under the table, Felicity was holding her nose while Sara squirmed to save her skull from cracking on the tabletop.

"Felix, your feet smell," Felicity complained in muffled, disgusted whisper.

"And you're on my leg, Felicity. Move over."

"Sorry, Sara."

Felicity managed to get off Sara's shin while Felix, who was smallest and therefore suffering the most, only wanted to know if the maitre d' had gone yet. Sara ventured a peep from under the cloth just in time to catch Mrs. Tarbush leaning confidentially toward Wellington Campbell. Their table was only a few feet away from the children and had been the goal of Sara's march across the dining room.

"I was hesitant to contact you, Mr. Campbell," Mrs. Tarbush breathed, "but when I read that you were looking for property in Avonlea, I couldn't help but think that it was Providence that our paths should cross once again."

Mr. Campbell looked rather doubtful about this and kept his gaze fixed on his lobster bisque.

"Well, I don't know about—"

"It is one of the most desirable properties on the Island, you know."

Mrs. Tarbush's fluttering eyelashes declared that she also included herself in that category.

"It is indeed beautiful," Mr. Campbell agreed, still not taking his eyes from his plate lest he be forced to read the woman's gaze.

"If I have to sell it, I would like the new owner to be somebody I know and trust."

"I'm flattered you thought of me, but I'm not sure..."

Mr. Campbell was getting the look of a man striving mightily to remain polite. Increased demands on one's reserves of politeness were among the pitfalls of wealth and public notice, Mr. Campbell knew. He also knew that he had fallen into the hands of a persistent woman, and there was nothing for it but to hear her out.

"A man of your distinction and stature," Mrs. Tarbush cut in, "deserves to have such a farm—a haven where you can rest and enjoy the company..."

Mr. Campbell was saved from the remainder of this thought by the sudden appearance of Sara, Felicity and Felix beside his table. The maitre d' had stepped out of the dining room, and Sara knew she had to seize the moment. She had jerked her companions out from their hiding place behind her. They all stood breathless now, trying to compose themselves and not look as though they had been crouching under tables. Taking a deep breath, Sara plunged straight into the topic at hand. She had to get Mr. Campbell on her side before the maitre d' spotted intruders.

"Excuse me, Mr. Wellington Campbell? We've come to ask you for a charitable donation to a cause I'm sure a man of your renown would agree with."

Wellington Campbell, taken by surprise,

began to frown. A gentleman of means was assailed by charitable appeals every second day. And he was not only on holiday here, he was also trying very hard to get a clear run at his lunch.

"Now look here, I'm not in—"

Mrs. Tarbush laughed lightly and tapped Mr. Campbell on the wrist with her fingers. The last thing she wanted was to have him jolted out of his benevolent mood.

"Wellington, the children are so earnest. What is it you want, my dears?"

Sara would take any ally she could get. Ever watchful for the maitre d', she hurried on with her speech. She had rehearsed it in her head all the way over and thought she knew just how to touch Mr. Campbell's soft spot.

"We are collecting for the Avonlea Public School library. The books there are the same ones as when you attended, Mr. Campbell. You can imagine—"

"Excuse me, young man."

A waiter bearing a cut-crystal water jug edged past Felix, frowning a little at all the young bodies standing in his way. The sight of him so unnerved Felix that the boy jumped back involuntarily just as the waiter bent to fill Mr. Campbell's water glass. Water went flying all over the tablecloth, into Mrs. Tarbush's lap and into the lobster bisque.

Mrs. Tarbush emitted a high-pitched squawk of dismay. Sara and Felicity whirled on the culprit.

"Felix!" they cried simultaneously.

"It was an a-accident."

It certainly was. Just the sort of accident to bring the dreaded maitre d' swooping down on them like a bat on its prey. He gripped Sara by the arm with one hand and Felicity with the other. Felix had already turned to jelly at the sight of the man's thunderous glare.

"I'm sorry, Mr. Campbell," the maitre d' apologized. "I thought you knew these children. I assure you, you'll not be disturbed again. This way, you little troublemakers!"

Even as the waiter rushed to mop up the spill, the maitre d' frog-marched the three invaders down the centre of the dining room, breathing heavily as he went. Burning to the roots of her hair, Sara tried to struggle, but she might as well have been a kitten in the man's iron grip.

"I'll have you know I've never been treated in such a fashion in my life!" she protested vehemently, even as a whole tableful of diners snickered at her plight.

The maitre d' propelled them out of the dining room and thrust them into the lobby. Finally

freed of his grip, they nearly staggered into a bust
of Queen Victoria, which glowered disapproving-
ly from a gilded pedestal.

"If you ever darken these doors again, you'll
have the authorities to answer to!" their tormen-
tor flung after them.

They barely had time to right themselves
before they found they had fallen straight into the
manager's clutches. The manager was even more
put out than the snooty maitre d'.

"I thought I told the lot of you to clear off!
Now get out and stay out!"

Before he could actually lay his hands on
them, the three children bolted out the front door
and onto the drive. Of course, Felix fell on his
face right in front of a rearing carriage horse.
Felicity and Sara hauled him to his feet and took
off with him at a dead run. Not until they were
safe in the high, wild grasses of the dunes did
they dare stop to gasp for breath and look fearful-
ly behind them.

When they found they had no pursuers, they
struggled to recover a few scraps of composure.
All Sara could think about was Mr. Wellington
Campbell sitting at that table, his pockets full of
money and not even allowed to hear her full
appeal. So much trouble, all for nothing!

"Felix, how could you be so clumsy? He was

ready to give us a donation," Sara rebuked.

Felix looked glad to have escaped with his life. Felicity, however, had turned a hot, indignant scarlet. She turned burning eyes upon her cousin.

"Well, Miss Sara Stanley, I have never been so humiliated in all my life, but I suppose you have been thrown out of much grander hotels than this!"

Felicity's pride was injured to the point where she supposed it might never recover. Even Felix felt sympathy for her. He turned his own flushed face to Sara.

"You and your great ideas. First you ruin the magic lantern show—"

"—and then you drag me around begging from door to door," Felicity slashed in, too outraged to let Felix have his full say. "I honestly don't know why we even bother listening to you."

Felix closed ranks, only knowing he had been enticed into a horrible adventure by a cousin he had hardly heard of a few weeks before. Better he get away from her now before she thought up something even worse to do to him. "Come on, Felicity, we can do better by ourselves."

Without another word, Felix and Felicity dashed off down the beach together, leaving poor Sara to make her way back alone.

Chapter Four

Ordinarily, the maple woods would have held all sorts of tempting delights for Sara. After growing up among the houses and pavements of the city, Sara had fallen in love with the maple woods, just as she had fallen in love with the countryside in general. She hadn't known there was air so clear it felt like breathing sparkles. She'd never seen ferns nearly as tall as herself, or watched chipmunks clowning on top of rocks, flicking their tails at her. She had never before sampled the pleasures of just lounging on an old mossy log and dreaming the hours away.

Today, as she trudged along the old sugar trail the teams used in the spring when the sap was running, all these same lures sang out to her. That Sara was deaf to their call was an indication of just how heavy was the load crushing down on her heart. Oh, it was dreadful to be the cause of doing a whole school out of its new books. Each of her efforts to make reparations had ended in disaster, and Sara could see there was no way she was ever going to collect another cent. The blight of it, she felt, was going to scourge her soul for years. And because of it, she was going to remain nothing but a laughingstock in Avonlea.

These gloomy thoughts so occupied her that she didn't see the man with the camera until she was almost upon him. Or rather, she saw half of the man. The other half was bent over and completely covered by the black cloth photographers flung over themselves and their cameras to block out the light. The man appeared to be fussing and fidgeting with something under there, and he had no idea Sara was watching.

If Sara had more bright ideas than three ordinary girls, she had more curiosity than five. For a minute, she actually forgot all about the school library fund as she paused to take in this strange spectacle. She had only seen photographers at work inside studios. She had no idea they ever simply took their cameras and roamed the wilds.

After a few moments, though, Sara grew uncomfortable about watching someone who didn't know she was there. It was very rude. And Sara was nothing if not polite.

"Hello," she called, when the man's head seemed about to emerge from under the cloth.

Sara's voice might as well have been a gunshot fired off behind the man's head. He jerked upright and stared about him. Sara could see he was tall and thin, and that his jacket was much too large for him. As soon as he spotted Sara poised next to a clump of birches, he stood stock-

still, looking like nothing so much as a huge, startled jackrabbit. He acted like a jackrabbit, too.
When Sara took a step toward him, he gathered
up his camera and tripod in a single motion and
started toward the field opposite, loping awk-
wardly but very fast under the load. Sara ran to
where the camera had been standing.

"What are you doing?" she cried. "Wait, come
back! Where are you going?"

Having a grown-up run away from her was
such a strange experience that Sara at once took
off after him. She thought this might be the fellow
she had glimpsed once or twice in Avonlea,
though he had always flitted behind some building before she could get a good look. "Oh,"
Felicity had tossed off, "that's the Awkward Man.
Nobody ever gets close to him."

The man had almost disappeared by the time
Sara reached the fence over which he'd leaped
with a single bound. His hat lay in the grass and
Sara scooped it up.

"You left your hat behind!" she called. All this
did was make the fellow gallop faster. He was so
busy trying to hang onto the camera and keep the
tripod from catching in the bushes that the camera cloth snagged on a twig and went sailing off
behind him. He didn't stop for the cloth any more
than he had for his hat.

"Stop! Please don't go!"

Sara jumped over the fence and started after him, amazed that a grown man seemed actually afraid of her. Grabbing the camera cloth, she emerged from the bushes just in time to see the fellow disappearing into an old barn on the other side of the strip of overgrown pasture in front of her.

"You dropped your cloth. Wait! Mister! Come back! What are you afraid of?"

Whatever it was, the fellow wasn't saying—unless he'd heard about the library fund and was making sure he didn't fall into Sara's clutches.

In exasperation, Sara paused, then sped on again. Now that she had the man's hat in her hand, there seemed nothing for it but to collect the cloth, too. He probably didn't even know he'd dropped them. Since Sara had started him running, the least she could do was save him a weary search in the underbrush.

By the time Sarah puffed up to the barn there wasn't a trace of the man, even though the barn door was swinging open on the breeze. Cautiously, Sara poked her head inside and listened. There was no sound, save for the pigeons cooing in the loft. Maybe the fellow had suffered a heart attack from fright, Sara thought. Or maybe he'd been a figment of her imagination.

Then Sara spotted a second open door and let out a breath. Her quarry was, no doubt, long gone out the other side of the building, and there wasn't any point in chasing after him. She would just set down the hat and cloth.

Now her eyes had adjusted to the darkness inside the barn, and she saw it had all been fixed over into some kind of workshop. Curious bits of metal and pieces of machinery stood about, and at the far end was a sealed room. Sara could no more resist a sealed room than a magpie could resist a piece of silver winking in the grass.

She took a step inside the barn, meaning merely to have a look at that sealed door. A sudden shuffle startled her. There stood the man, not five feet away, staring at Sara as though she were a fire-breathing dragon about to gobble him whole.

"You dropped your hat and cloth," she explained quickly, lest he bolt on her again. She felt she should put the items down and back away, as one did with bread crumbs when trying to entice a wild squirrel to eat from one's hand.

When the photographer didn't move or speak, Sara realized that he was indeed the Awkward Man, a sort of local legend around Avonlea. He lived by himself and had as little to do with people as possible. His monthly trips to the general store were an agony to him, and when people tried to speak, he only swallowed hard and ducked into a doorway. Though it was accepted that the Awkward Man could fix just about anything, newfangled or old, what he did out here and how he spent his time were generally a mystery.

"Allow me to introduce myself," said Sara, who saw she would have to do the talking. "My name is Sara Stanley. What's yours?"

At first, she thought he might be lacking the power of speech altogether. Then he managed to open his mouth.

"Jasper...D-dale. Now, p-please, I would...like to b-be left alone."

At once, Sara understood part of the reason the man was a recluse. Getting each word out seemed as much effort to him as pushing a boulder uphill. He was afflicted with the most unsettling stutter.

"All right, if you really want me to," Sara answered, more intrigued by the second and determined to stay if she could.

Somehow, she had imagined the Awkward Man as old and wizened and probably crazy. Yet this man had turned out to be almost young—well, certainly no older than Aunt Olivia, anyway. And nice-looking too, if he would only stop scowling. He had reddish hair that needed a cut and an Adam's apple that bobbed up and down nervously. He had a name, too. Jasper Dale. It sounded quite poetic to Sara's ears.

"Y-yes," Jasper sputtered. "Please do."

He sidled past Sara into the room she had previously noticed and closed the door again with a slam. If that wasn't a hint to leave, Sara didn't know what was. Just as she was looking for some place to lay down the hat and cloth, which she was still holding, she was startled by an enormous crash from inside the room. Thinking Jasper Dale certainly crushed beneath a whole wagonload of mechanical bits and pieces, Sara rushed over and yanked open the door. She found Jasper on his knees in the midst of pans and trays and strange-looking gadgets, which he was trying frantically to gather up.

"Mr. Dale, are you all right? Can I help you?"

"No. Just...g-go away."

Jasper's face was contorted with embarrassment, and everything he picked up, he contrived to drop again. Forgetting the gadgets, he suddenly retrieved his hat and cloth from Sara and shut the door almost on her nose. A little angry now, Sara boldly opened the door again, and stood firmly on the sill. Now she realized what the room was: some kind of photographic workroom.

She had stumbled across one of Jasper Dale's secrets.

Jasper didn't take kindly to her intrusion.

"C-close the door. Take my advice and leave. You shouldn't follow p-people you don't know into b-barns."

"If only I could take everyone's advice and not run so headlong into things. Aunt Hetty says I'm unstoppable."

Jasper looked as though he agreed. He turned his back to Sara and started busily mixing up some sort of chemical solution.

"Just g-go. I'm very busy. I can't have anyone around when I'm d-developing plates."

His mistake was to mention plates. Sara, perhaps due to her shattering experience with Mr. Beatty, was gripped by a deep fascination with photographic plates of any kind.

"Please, can't I stay? I've always wanted to see how it's done. I'll stay out of your way."

Jasper looked at her in dismay but didn't seem to be able to think of any way to get her to leave.

"Oh, all right...uh...uh stay," he mumbled. "But close the d-door. I've got to h-have darkness."

"You have some amazing things in here, Mr. Dale," Sara commented as she complied. Then, since Jasper Dale gave no sign of hearing her, she fell into silence, climbing up on a stool and sitting still as a mouse while Jasper worked.

Whatever he was doing seemed to take a dreadfully long time, but the reward was certainly worth the wait. Setting an oil lamp into a projector, Jasper lifted a newly developed slide from the pan and slid it into place. Magically, a large photograph appeared on the opposite wall. It was of Sara, hovering on the edge of the maple woods, her hair floating in the breeze, her eyes alive with interest as she looked directly toward what must have been Jasper Dale's camera. Sara was completely in awe.

"It's so beautiful. That's me."

Jasper gave an uneasy hitch, as though he had just then realized this fact too.

"Oh, s-sorry. I d-didn't realize I had t-taken your photograph."

Sara continued to be transfixed by the image. She couldn't possibly have imagined what it would be like to see her own picture blown up on the wall like that. "It's a very strange experience to see myself so large. I usually feel so small."

Perhaps all of Sara's recent humiliations in Avonlea were in her voice as she spoke. Perhaps there was just a trace of how forlorn she sometimes felt at still being a stranger in the small community. For the first time, Jasper Dale seemed to stop quaking. He looked at Sara with large, brown, bespectacled eyes, as though he knew precisely what she meant.

"It's a magic lantern," he told her, an edge of pride creeping in. "F-finest one on the Island."

Of course, he could have had no idea what the words "magic lantern" meant to Sara Stanley. She rose up from the stool on which she had been sitting, her eyes huge with possibilities.

"Do you have any other slides?" she asked breathlessly.

"Yep."

Unsuspectingly, Jasper hefted down a box from a shelf and handed it to Sara, who dived in and started looking. Several moments later, glowing all over, she emerged from her examination.

"There are dozens of them. Has anyone ever seen them?"

"No."

Sara stood up, clasped her hands together and gazed at Jasper Dale full in the face.

"Mr. Dale," she said slowly, "I have a great favor to ask you. Would you help me put on a magic lantern show?"

If she had asked Jasper Dale to jump head first off a thousand-foot cliff, he could not have been more alarmed. "No," he choked out in panic. "I d-don't really think I could help you."

Sara's appealing gaze never wavered. And when Sara wanted to appeal to someone, she put everything she had into it.

"But you don't understand. You see, I've let everybody down."

Her tone was laced with such tragic meaning that Jasper managed to get a hold of himself.

"You're m-much too young to have let anyone d-down." The merest, faintest hint of humor touched his mouth.

"Oh, but I have." Sara exposed her full infamy. "I'm the one who helped Mr. Beatty escape with all the money for the library fund. The whole town is talking about me."

"Avonlea might talk for a while, but they'll get over it."

Jasper sounded as though he had close acquaintance with just how much Avonlea talked.

"But I won't. I want them to like me."

There! It was out! Sara had never realized until she actually said it aloud how desperately she wanted to belong in Avonlea. A complete stranger, Sara had been dropped among all sorts of confusing relatives she had never seen before. Now she had grown to love them, and love the village. But how could she ever truly be accepted with a scandal like the stolen library fund forever

hanging over her head. So much sympathy flood-
ed into Jasper Dale's face that he actually looked
as though he were going to smile. His mouth
worked at it a moment before he spoke.

"You really think a m-magic lantern show
would do the trick?" he ventured.

"It would work...well, like magic! But I can't
do it without you."

Well, here was someone needing Jasper Dale
and needing him badly, to judge from the plea on
her face. This was something that hadn't happened to Jasper in many years. Timid though he
was, he just couldn't resist. His Adam's apple
jumped and he brushed distractedly at hair that
wasn't in his eyes.

"Well...if you don't th-think I'll get in the
way."

"Get in the way?" Sara cried. "Mr. Dale, it was
fate that we met this afternoon!"

Chapter Five

Winning the support of Jasper Dale proved to
be the easiest part of the plan. There was, after all,
Aunt Hetty to convince, and the sooner the better.

Girding herself to face this formidable obstacle,
Sara spent all afternoon thinking up persuasive

speeches. That evening, she was on her best behavior—passing Aunt Hetty everything first at dinner, jumping up afterwards to wash the dishes. After she supposed she had Aunt Hetty softened up as much she was going to be softened, Sara broke her news about a new magic lantern show. Before she was able to get even one argument out in its favor, Aunt Hetty was sputtering and waving her hands.

"Magic lantern show! Sara Stanley, are you dreaming? If I hear one more thing about—"

"Jasper Dale has a magic lantern," Sara got out, trying to forestall objections with this piece of information. A magic lantern so close at hand seemed a tremendous selling point.

"Jasper Dale!" Aunt Hetty scoffed. "That man hasn't said a peep to anyone in this town for years."

But at least, Sara thought privately, he wasn't likely to light out in a stolen horse and buggy.

"He promised to help me. Please, Aunt Hetty. I know I can do it."

"It's totally out of the question. I've already been down that road and been made an absolute fool of in the process."

She spoke as though Mr. Beatty had fled with the library funds just to make a fool of Hetty King.

"But there won't be enough money to buy

books," Sara argued, appealing to the guardian of culture in her aunt. "We have to do something."

Did Aunt Hetty want the children of Avonlea growing up as illiterate savages? Sara's gaze asked silently.

"It was a popular idea, Hetty," added Olivia, rallying to Sara's cause. "I feel that—"

"You feel!" Aunt Hetty impaled Olivia with a reproving glare. "It's about time you started to think, Olivia, not just feel. What's doomed to failure once is doomed to failure twice."

With this thudding pronouncement, Hetty went off to work on the seventh-grade composition papers, leaving Sara with the pile of dishes and Olivia with red spots staining her cheeks. Sara and Olivia exchanged a look that said, in one moment, everything there was to say about Aunt Hetty.

Then, with the air of one battered veteran acknowledging another, Olivia grinned. Sara grinned back. She had Olivia on her side, at least. Sara applied herself to the dishpan with renewed will. In no way did she intend to give up on what she regarded as her only chance to redeem her honor in the eyes of Avonlea.

Olivia proved a staunch ally. During the following days, she and Sara exercised such reason,

persuasion and sheer persistence on Aunt Hetty
that finally the results appeared in the form of a
brand new poster on the general store bulletin
board. The poster read:

Back by Popular Demand!
A Magic Lantern show
in aid of the Avonlea School Library.
Narrated by Miss Sara Stanley.
Operated by Mr. Jasper Dale.
Saturday at six o'clock.
Avonlea Town Hall

When the poster went up, Olivia and Sara
flew straight to the general store to admire it.

"I still can't believe it," Olivia murmured.
"Hetty gave in. Of course, only success will justify it in her eyes." Olivia's quiet voice had played
a large part in Hetty's capitulation, and she was
secretly pleased with herself.

Of course, Hetty's consent had been accompanied by many dire predictions of failure. If listening to them was the price that had to be paid,
then Sara paid it willingly. Besides, like Clemmie
Ray, she wasn't above begging divine Providence
that none of them would come true.

Mr. Lawson strolled out of his store to admire
the poster too.

"Well, Sara Stanley, promise me you won't go
running off with the money this time."

Mr. Lawson was meaning to be funny, but Sara winced at the painful memory.

"Don't worry, Mr. Lawson, I aim to make this a show to remember."

Sara meant this to the tips of her toes. The magic lantern show would be a whopping success, even if she had to die in the attempt. Mr. Lawson laughed at her earnestness.

"I'm sure it will be. Anyone who can get Jasper Dale to come out of hiding is bound to be full of surprises."

The store door slammed behind Mrs. Ray, Clemmie's mother, the very same lady who thought reading was the road to the devil. She was a large, bony woman who seemed a good match for Old Scratch himself and any little demons he cared to bring with him.

"Magic lantern show indeed!" She twitched her skirt to one side as she passed the offending poster. "I don't approve of picture shows, and I don't approve of library funds, neither. Hard work— that's what young people need more than books."

She looked as though she would have liked to put the entire youthful population of Avonlea to work hauling rocks that minute. Olivia slipped her hand protectively over Sara's.

"Well, I'm sure you're entitled to your opinion, Mrs. Ray."

Not trusting herself to continue being civil, Olivia led Sara briskly out of earshot and toward home. Mrs. Ray turned toward Sally Potts and her mother, who had come up to read the announcement.

"Trust a little chip from Montreal to come up with an idea like that. Look at her—walking along as if she owned the earth. Even if she has relations here, she's not a real Islander."

This was the ultimate insult in Avonlea and, luckily, Sara was not close enough to hear it. Sally Potts squinched up her eyes maliciously. Now that Sally had got wind of Sara Stanley's grandiose plan, she made up her mind to do all she could to thwart it.

"Jasper Dale—the Awkward Man," snorted Mrs. Potts. "He's as buggy as a bedbug."

Mrs. Ray jerked her bonnet in agreement. Where else would insanity be but at a magic lantern show?

"I was just saying as you won't find *me* there."

Picking up her basket, Mrs. Ray strode off, her footsteps kicking up little puffs of dust behind her. She left Mrs. Potts to smile rather nastily. Mrs. Potts was simply an adult copy of her daughter. It only took a glance to see where Sally had come by her unpleasantness.

"Mind you," Mrs. Potts jibed, "seeing Jasper

Dale in a crowd would be worth the price of admission."

Chapter Six

It was going to take a lot more than Jasper Dale to make the show worth the price of admission. As Sara quickly found out, there was an awful lot of work involved in putting on a public entertainment. She threw herself into it nevertheless, and saw that all her relatives did so too.

Besides printing the poster and seeing that news of the show reached every corner of Avonlea, the slides had to be selected and Jasper Dale's nerves kept smoothed. Then, on the day before the show, the Town Hall had to be got ready.

Sara managed to get everyone there early—even Jasper Dale. Stumbling in with a great armload of equipment, he rushed straight up to the balcony where he could work safely, unseen. There, with only Andrew as a companion, he set up the magic lantern . Andrew, as usual, was fascinated by the new contraption. He picked up a few slides and slid them in, one after another.

"I see how it works. So, this one disappears just as this one reappears on the screen."

"Yes," mumbled Jasper, "as long as your p-pictures are set up right."

"Ok, well, can I try it?"

"Yep."

Jasper didn't seem to mind that Andrew was fiddling with the precious magic lantern. In fact, he seemed exceedingly pleased that someone was taking an interest in its operation. Andrew looked in both ends of the ornately painted box, then held the oil lamp behind it.

"Is this what turns it on?"

"Y-yep."

With each word, Jasper was backing a little more toward the balcony stairs, failing to notice that he was being observed by Hetty and Olivia. The two women were teetering on chairs at the front of the hall, trying to hang the white bed-sheet on which the slides would be shown. Not far away, Mrs. Lawson was trying out the piano, for what was a magic lantern show without spine-tingling musical accompaniment? Mrs. Lawson frowned at the instrument, which was a battered survivor of countless Town Hall events and doing its tinny best.

"Either the piano's out of tune or I'm out of practice."

She thumped out another cord. Sara had been most particular about the music, and Mrs. Lawson wanted to give it her best. She turned to the stage for a second opinion, but Hetty and

Olivia were too busy peering sideways at the balcony.

"Imagine Jasper Dale having anything to do with a magic lantern show," chuckled Olivia, still impressed that Sara had drawn Avonlea's shiest hermit out of hiding.

"Imagine Hetty King having anything to do with one, either, Olivia. Well, I feel that you and that child will be the death of me."

Hetty banged in a tack as though she felt the death pangs coming upon her already. She could not forget how she had been bamboozled by Mr. Beatty. How could Olivia hum at her task, so foolishly oblivious to the catastrophe stalking their family name?

On the balcony, Andrew, a most clever boy, was learning rapidly. Aunt Hetty had high hopes he would one day go to university.

"I just slide this in here..."

"Yep." Edging backward, Jasper had almost made it to the first stair now. Andrew hadn't so much as noticed. "But do it c-carefully, 'cause they're f-fragile."

"Okay."

Nervously, Jasper peeped over the balcony. The main hall was empty, his way was clear. That was all Jasper needed. With a gulp, he grabbed his hat and sped down the balcony staircase.

Andrew, totally unaware of his mentor's defection, peered into the front of the magic lantern again.

"Mr. Dale, how do you know if a slide's upside down? Mr Dale?"

But all that was left of Jasper Dale was the echo of his boots and the box of slides he and Sara had so carefully organized.

Unfortunately, Jasper didn't make a clean getaway. Sara and Felicity, unstacking chairs, were between him and the outer door.

"I don't know why you would strike up a friendship with the Awkward Man, of all people, Sara," Felicity was saying. She was not happy about being dragooned into helping with the slide show, and especially not happy about so much bustling activity being all Sara's idea.

"Don't call him the Awkward Man. He's just a little shy. If you got to know him, you'd find he's a very clever man."

Sara always defended her friends, new or old, and she liked Jasper Dale tremendously, in spite of the man's difficulty in getting out two full sentences together. She understood what bravery it had taken for Jasper to attempt the magic lantern show, and a plan had already begun to form in her mind. If she could just get Jasper through all this in one piece, he would be able to taste the

Magically, a large photograph appeared on the opposite wall. It was of Sara, hovering on the edge of the maple woods, her hair floating on the breeze. Sara was completely in awe.

"I want you to know," Sara told Jasper sincerely, "that we couldn't have done it without you, Mr. Dale. Thank you for not letting me down."

"Why is he hiding from me?" she wanted to know. Had she, personally, done something to upset the man?

Olivia only smiled. "It is not just you, Sara. Jasper Dale's been like that for a long time."

sweet taste of success. Once tasted, success would bring him out a second time more easily. Pretty soon, a transformed Jasper Dale...

Felicity, who admired grace and self-possession above all else, let out a sharp "Humph! He may be clever," she huffed, "but he can't even walk without tripping over his own feet."

At that precise moment, that's exactly what Jasper did, drawing the attention of both the girls. Sara rushed over.

"Mr. Dale, where are you going?"

Jasper stood there, graceless in baggy trousers, rumpled coat and wire-rimmed spectacles almost falling off the end of his nose. "Um, it's, it's all s-set up, so I, uh, guess I'll be g-going."

"You're coming back for the show, aren't you?" Sara asked anxiously. She didn't like the way he had begun to shuffle from foot to foot and look longingly toward the door.

"Andrew c-can run the lantern. I mean, he kn-knows how."

Sara saw her plan utterly ruined if Jasper didn't come for the show.

"Mr. Dale, you promised!"

Sara managed to pack every scrap of her expectations into those few little words. Jasper peered helplessly at her, trying to find some way to convey his total terror of crowds. The more

badly he needed words, the worse they deserted
him.

"Oh, uh, I don't, I don't, I d-don't..."

"Please, Mr. Dale, we're partners."

Sticking out her hand, Sara took Jasper's in a
grip that no general inspiring the troops could
have made firmer. The show, her gaze insisted,
couldn't possibly go on without him. Jasper
ducked his head, torn between a desire to please
Sara and an overwhelming urge to flee.

"Oh, well..."

Hetty, Olivia and Mrs. Lawson came in from
the main hall. Before Jasper knew what was hap-
pening, he was surrounded. Sara spoke quickly.

"You must meet my aunts. This is Aunt Olivia
and this is Aunt Hetty."

Jasper looked like a turtle, trying to disappear
inside his own clothes. His spectacles quivered
and he seemed unable to lift his gaze beyond
Hetty's knees. Of course, being confronted by
Avonlea's outspoken schoolmistress was a bit of a
trial for anyone, as Jasper soon found out. Trust
Aunt Hetty to get right to his sore point.

"Hello Jasper," she rasped out. "I hope you
won't run off before the show as our infamous
Mr. Beatty did."

"Mr. Dale would never do that," Sara asserted
sturdily, daring to give her aunt a reproachful

stare. Jasper didn't help by suddenly remembering to snatch off his hat and crumple it in a death-
grip against his chest.

The very picture of grim doubt, Hetty nodded
and continued grandly on her way. Olivia stayed,
though, smiling kindly at Jasper.

"Thank you for helping the cause, Jasper. I
know the show will live up to everyone's expectations."

Jasper's jaw worked but speech had completely abandoned him. His ears burned like beacons
as he made a fumbling attempt to shake Olivia's
hand.

"Well, well, Mr. Dale," exclaimed Mrs.
Lawson, quite agog with curiosity at seeing
Jasper taking part in a village activity. "You are a
most secretive man. We always knew that you
were mechanically inclined, but who would have
guessed you could turn your talents to such a
lovely entertainment?"

Mrs. Lawson meant well, but she so distracted
Jasper that he forgot to let go of Olivia's hand.
When he finally realized he was still clutching it,
he let go as though he had been holding a hot
potato and hightailed it toward the door.

Just outside, Felix was on a ladder with a
paintbrush, doing his bit to spruce up the building. Sally Potts, missing nothing that went on in

Avonlea, had just strolled over to the hall for the express purpose of ridiculing the upcoming show.

"What Sara won't do to earn a little money," she scoffed, squinting coldly up at Felix. "What a little show-off!"

"You're just jealous," flared Peter Craig, who was holding the ladder. His accuracy drew Sally's venom upon himself.

"You'd think you were *her* hired boy, Peter Craig, the way she's got you like a toad on a string!"

At that moment, Jasper Dale burst into the sunshine and began to lope up the road. From behind, he seemed to be constructed of nothing but bony limbs and knobby joints, with none of the joints fitting together right. Seeing another victim, Sally Potts was after him in an instant. From behind the cover of a lilac bush, she shouted rudely at the top of her lungs.

"Jasper Dale! Jasper Dale! Likes to hide in a garbage pail!"

Jasper's contorted face revealed that he had heard every word and was embarrassed beyond belief. His ears turned from pink to flaming scarlet, and he lost his hat again as he started to run, Sally's laughter ringing in his ears. Felix put down his paintbrush.

"Next to Sally Potts, Felicity's a saint," he muttered under his breath.

When the hall had been pretty well put to rights and dinnertime approached, Sara and Olivia set out walking along the road home. Though Sara hadn't seen the episode between Jasper and Sally Potts, she had had enough experience herself with his strange behavior to be thoroughly puzzled. Now that she had Aunt Olivia to herself, she hoped to solve the mystery of Jasper Dale.

"Why is he hiding from me?" she wanted to know. Had she, personally, done something to upset the man?

Olivia only smiled.

"It's not just you, Sara. Jasper Dale's been like that for a long time."

"But why?"

Olivia sighed softly.

"A lot of reasons, I guess. I remember when he was young. His parents had such high expectations of him that, no matter how hard he tried, he just could never please them."

This made Sara think immediately of Aunt Hetty.

"How awful."

"And then, when he was grown-up and his

mother took sick, Addie McNeil was sent to nurse her, and Jasper fell madly in love with her, but his mother just wouldn't consent to their marriage, even on her deathbed."

His mother had refused his heart's desire! Even from her deathbed! Sara's mouth fell open into a round, pink "O." If Jasper had been seared by the fires of tragic love, no wonder he had given up on the world.

"How could she?" Sara cried, unable to imagine such hard heartedness.

Olivia shrugged. "Well, Jasper rebelled and he arranged to be married. Anyway, even from the grave his mother won out. The wedding day arrived and the bride didn't. She ran away with a farmer from the next concession. She jilted Jasper at the altar, in front of the whole town."

"Poor Jasper!"

Sara's own troubles shrank clean away by comparison. Jasper's ordeal had been far worse than publicly helping a thief run away with the library funds.

"He's been a recluse ever since," Olivia finished.

Sara could understand that perfectly well. She had had strong reclusive impulses herself the day after Mr. Beatty had taken to his heels. Why, if something wasn't done, Jasper Dale was liable to languish his whole life away hiding in his house or his barn. How fortunate that Sara had talked him into doing the magic lantern show. That would be the saving of him. Success would show Jasper how understanding folks could be. The magic lantern would make him a hero in front of all Avonlea.

Chapter Seven

Though the evening of the magic lantern show finally arrived, not all residents of Avonlea planned to attend. The Ray children, for instance, were condemned to stay at home. Their mother went even further than that. As though to remove herself entirely from the contamination of such dangerous frivolity, Mrs. Ray had hitched up the buggy. She meant to drive all the way over to Newbridge and spend the night with her sister. Young Clemmie was being left in the charge of her older brother, Edward, an arrangement Clemmie didn't care for at all. She dragged her feet as she followed Edward down to the gate to wave goodbye to their mother.

"Bye Clemmie," Mrs. Ray called out, giving Clemmie's woeful face one last stern look as she whipped the horse up smartly. "Be good, Edward."

There wasn't much chance of that. The minute the buggy was rattling off past the cornfield, Edward picked up a small rock and pitched it deliberately into the dust at Clemmie's feet.

"I told you Ma would never let you go to that stupid show."

Clemmie hunched her shoulders, knowing Edward was going to be mean. And she longed, with all her heart, to go to the magic lantern show.

"It's not fair. I don't know anyone who has the measles. Everyone else is going!"

The threat of catching this dread disease was the reason Mrs. Ray had given for forbidding her children to go. Tears were already starting up in Clemmie's eyes but they didn't have the least sway over Edward. His little sister was always howling, and he intended to have none of it. He only made sure the buggy was out of earshot before turning his back.

"I'm going to meet Fred Bell in the woods," he announced. "We built a fort, and we're going to sleep there all night. We planned this the whole summer."

"But you're supposed to take care of me while Ma's gone," Clemmie protested in alarm. A mean brother was better than no brother at all when you were left to fend for yourself on a lonely farm.

"I got better things to do."

Edward started to walk away. Desperate, Clemmie resorted at once to her most drastic threat.

"I'll tell Ma!"

Instantly, Edward was upon her, twisting her arm roughly behind her back. He was almost twice as big as Clemmie and all hard elbows and snarl.

"You tell and I'll bury you in the backyard with the ants and they'll bite you and get in your ears and in your nose."

Clemmie, who was young enough to believe what big boys told her, imagined huge pincers snapping off her nose and shredding her ears—all while she was buried alive in the cold, icky dirt. Her breath caught in great sobs in her throat.

"Stop it, Edward," she wailed pathetically. "Stop!"

With a final twist to make sure Clemmie got the point, Edward let go of her. Snickering, he strolled off toward the woods, leaving Clemmie plopped down on the grass, rubbing her arm and hiccuping miserably.

Back at Rose Cottage, where Sara lived, things were in a much different state. For ages, it seemed, the house had been filled with rush and flurry as everyone got ready for the magic lantern show. When one was accountable for such a large undertaking, Sara discovered, a thousand and one unexpected details had to be taken care of. Sara lost her notes about the order of the slides, then found them again tucked inside her hatband. Aunt Olivia couldn't remember whether or not Mrs. Lawson had been told about the march she was to play when Sara made her entrance. Aunt Hetty discovered that it was one of her finest linen bedsheets they had nailed up in the hall, and not the second-best cotton one as she'd supposed.

The King family meant to go in force, and, to that end, Uncle Alec and Aunt Janet drew up in their buggy that evening at the door of Rose Cottage. Hetty came out and got up behind them, followed by Olivia. Hetty had insisted on wearing her dark brown serge, which doubled as her funeral-going dress, in case the evening turned out to be a disaster.

A second buggy, driven by Peter, was pulled up behind, assigned to carry the children. Andrew, Felicity, Felix and Cecily were already perched on the seats. Felicity had got to wear her pink muslin at last. She was much occupied with smoothing the pleats and keeping the hem out of range of Felix's boots. Everyone's nerves were humming.

"Where is Sara?" Hetty grumbled. "That girl is slower than molasses in January."

Sara wasn't slow. She was working hard at making herself as striking as she could. If the magic lantern showed the pictures, it was Sara who must tell their tale. As narrator, she would stand all evening at the edge of the stage, every eye upon her, as she took the audience through the show she had prepared. She had to rise to the task—not only for herself, the library fund and skeptical Aunt Hetty—most of all, she felt she owed her finest effort to Jasper Dale.

When Sara finally emerged from Rose Cottage, everyone outside was speechless. The dress she wore was pale as new ivory and it trailed behind her in long, shimmering folds edged everywhere with real Valenciennes lace. Her blond hair was pinned high up on her head and entwined with a crown of freshly picked flowers. The effect she strove for was of some sylphlike spirit who had descended into the Avonlea Town Hall from another world.

Even Felicity was taken aback, though she wasn't going to show it. Her gaze skimmed Sara up and down.

"I shouldn't think you would wear that, Sara. Those flowers will wilt in the heat."

Ignoring Felicity, Sara climbed up on the

buggy and took her seat with the grace of an archduchess ascending her throne. Mood! Mood was everything. Sara had worked herself up into a state of elevated feeling which she would not allow to be broken until every bit of the narration was done.

Among the adults, there were a good many raised eyebrows and twitching lips, but every one of them managed to hold their tongues. Finally, Uncle Alec clucked to the horse. "We're off then."

The grown-ups rumbled off at a good clip down the road.

"Don't dilly-dally now," Aunt Janet called over her shoulder. "We'll see you there." Peter started up the second buggy—at a slower pace since it was considerably overcrowded. Besides, being the driver gave Peter a grave responsibility. He didn't dare let it get too windy, or get any road dust on Sara.

"Aren't you nervous about getting up in front of all those people?" Cecily asked when they had nicely got going. Cecily hadn't been able to take her eyes off Sara's outfit. She was overawed that Sara was going to stand on the Town Hall stage and speak.

"Yes, a little bit," Sara admitted, coming temporarily down from her cloud. In truth, she had a great flock of butterflies inside her, all struggling madly to get out. Every great artist, she had once read, suffered this way before stepping out into the lights and the applause.

Andrew gave her a comradely poke with his elbow.

"My father says that when you're going to speak in public, all you have to do is get it firm in your head that it's just a bunch of cabbage heads in the audience. Then you won't be nervous."

Felix giggled, but Sara drew herself up severely. Bad as her nerves were, she had much more ambitious goals in mind than just getting through her speech alive.

"I don't think there will be much inspiration in talking to cabbage heads. I want to speak to people and see them looking interested or thrilled."

"Or bored to tears," put in Felicity disparagingly, catching the starry look in Sara's eyes.

Sara paid no attention, knowing only that if she could manage to enthrall the village of Avonlea this evening, she would never ask another thing of her dramatic career. So wrapped up in her thoughts was Sara that no one else said anything until the buggy reached the Ray place. There, they found Clemmie huddled by the gate, afraid to go back into the house now that Edward wasn't there, and almost ready to start out for

Newbridge after her Ma. Peter pulled up the buggy.

"Whatever is the matter now, Clemmie?" Felicity asked impatiently.

Clemmie turned up a small, tear-stained face.

"Edward's left me all alone in the house, and Ma's forbidden me to go to the magic lantern show. She says Markdale's full of measles. And there's sure to be some Markdale people at the show."

Clemmie looked ready to risk the Black Plague if only she could go.

"I don't think there's any danger of catching the measles," Andrew said soothingly. "If there were, we wouldn't be allowed to go."

Sara saw part of her audience being forcibly kept away. She shook herself out of her reverie.

"Oh, Clemmie, surely if you tell your Ma that it's all right with all of our grown-ups..."

"It's too late. Ma's gone to Newbridge and she won't be back till tomorrow."

So! There was nobody in the house to do any more forbidding. Sara held out her hand.

"Well then, why don't you just come with us to the show anyhow? Your mother won't ever know."

That Sara wasn't above trying to outmanoeuvre the disagreeable Mrs. Ray shocked Felicity.

"Sara, you shouldn't put Clemmie up to disobeying her mother!"

"Felicity, you stay out of this!" Sara turned back to Clemmie, who was now clutching the gatepost as though it were her only friend in the world. "Now, look, Clemmie, go into this with all your heart if you go into it at all. There's no use doing something bad if you spoil your fun by wishing all the time that you were good."

The effect of this piece of philosophy was to start Clemmie wailing at the top of her lungs again. She may have wanted to enjoy being bad with all her heart, but there were the terrible consequences to be considered.

"What if Ma finds out?"

Sara let out an exaggerated sigh and straightened up again.

"If you're going to be scared, you'd better not come. Drive on, Peter."

The buggy started up. Five seconds later, so did Clemmie.

"Wait! I'm coming," she shrieked, flying down the road after them.

Peter stopped so that Clemmie could clamber hastily up beside Sara. Any amount of licking from her mother, or even a good case of the measles, was far better than being left in the dark, empty house alone all night.

Chapter Eight

As the buggy approached the village, Sara's chest grew tighter and tighter. What if everyone were still angry with her because of Mr. Beatty? What if everyone decided to think the way Mrs. Ray did about the magic lantern show?

What if no one came?

In this wrought-up state, Sara imagined in gruesome detail this final, ultimate catastrophe. It was quite possible, too! This time, to prevent any possibility of the funds disappearing before the show, no tickets had been sold ahead of time. Sara had no idea of how many people might actually come. In her heart, she had nursed a secret terror that only her cousins would tramp into the echoing Town Hall, and maybe dependable Mr. Lawson. He would *have* to come to hear his wife play piano.

As they rounded the last corner, Sara shut her eyes tight...

"Sara! Look!"

Cecily was tugging excitedly at Sara's sleeve and pointing. With a gulp, Sara peeped through her lashes—then her eyes flew open wide. The Town Hall was so crowded round with buggies that people could scarcely get past them to the door. Outside, men and women stood about in knots, greeting each other and chatting with all the holiday air of a midsummer picnic. Children, who had not forgotten how they had been cheated of a treat when Mr. Beatty fled, now hopped up and down with anticipation, scarcely able to wait for the show to begin.

Sara's heart began to thump very fast. Sometimes it's as scary a thing to meet an overwhelming success as it is to face disaster. As Peter drove the buggy round the side to where there was still room to tie up the horse, Sara saw that Hetty and Olivia were already at their posts by the door, collecting ticket money and nodding to people as they entered. That, at least, was a relief. With two such paragons guarding the cash-box, there was no chance whatever that the money would go anywhere but straight into the library fund.

At the door, Olivia beamed and smiled as the people streamed by her, her face flushed with pleasure. With Sara, she had worked very hard on the show. It was gratifying to see such results to her labors.

"My goodness, what a turn-out, Hetty," she whispered when she got a moment. "The library will be a huge success."

Hetty, who ought to have been the most

pleased with the rapidly filling hall, kept her mouth in a thin, rigid line. She was constitutionally unable to change her opinions on such short notice.

"Don't count your chickens. It isn't over yet." Lightning could still strike them down, or the roof fall in.

The very first thing Sara did when she got out of the buggy was to collect Jasper Dale from behind the general store where she had spotted him hovering, unable to approach the crowded Town Hall all by himself. It was a good thing she went, too. She found Jasper so nervous in his best jacket that he had practically hanged himself trying to knot his tie. Though she had to stand on a chair to do it, Sara got his tie straightened out and his jacket neatly buttoned.

"There! You really look very nice," she told him, truly meaning it. When Jasper Dale managed to stand still, he was quite a fine figure of a man.

They set out for the hall, with Jasper hesitating every few yards of the way. By the time Sara got him to the door, she felt like a sheepdog who had put the work of herding a whole flock into moving a single skittish sheep. Jasper's spectacles were already steaming up at the sight of the people, and Sara was sure his knees were shaking.

"Don't worry, Mr. Dale, everything will go all right."

Her efforts to brace Jasper had made Sara forget her own fears. Consequently, confidence seemed to radiate from her eager face. Even Jasper picked it up and began, daringly, to believe too.

"Good, S-Sara," he got out, actually letting her lead him up the Town Hall steps.

It was a good thing Sara was with him, for they ran into Sally Potts and her friend Jane just outside the door. After sneering at Jasper, Sally took in Sara's extravagant outfit and pulled her mouth into a prune. "You wouldn't catch *me* showing off in front of the whole town!"

Sara turned her crowned head regally. "Oh, is the whole town here?" she drawled. "Think of the money we will make."

Having neatly squelched Sally, Sara ushered Jasper inside and over to the foot of the balcony stairs where he could be disappear on his own up to his station. Jasper was standing straighter, she thought, and had actually nodded to a couple of surprised people. Oh, she just knew in her bones that her plan was going to work!

Sara wouldn't have been nearly so sure about that if she had been able to hear Sally and Jane. Sally's gaze had bored into Sara's back right up until Sara had disappeared inside. Jostled by the

crowd as she was, and seeing all the money flowing into Hetty and Olivia's hands, Sally knew the
evening was set to be a triumph for Sara Stanley.
And that Sally Potts could not bear.

She stood scowling for a long moment. Then a
wicked smile snaked across her lips.

"I bet it wouldn't take much to upset Sara's
little show, Jasper Dale being so jumpy and all."

Jane's eyes popped round as quarters.

"Sally Potts! You *wouldn't!*" Jane cried, completely and deliciously scandalized.

The two ran off just as the rest of the crowd
outside was distracted by the arrival of a grand
conveyance boasting lacquered panels, a fringed
canopy and a pair of high-stepping horses. The
vehicle carried none other than Mr. Wellington
Campbell himself, accompanied, inevitably, by
Mrs. Tarbush. Mr. Campbell lifted Mrs. Tarbush
down, not five feet from where Aunt Janet and
Uncle Alec stood talking to their neighbors.

"We were beginning to think you were too
good for the Island, Mr. Campbell," commented
Aunt Janet, her tone only half humorous. She
hadn't failed to notice that Mr. Campbell was
resplendent in a fine-fitting black coat, certainly not
tailored locally. He also sported a silk tie and a gold
stickpin, with what looked like a real diamond in it.
And nowhere was there evidence of sweat.

"Oh, Wellington isn't nearly as unapproach-able as the papers make him out to be."

Despite Wellington's raised eyebrows, Mrs. Tarbush seemed to consider herself an authority in this matter. She had been working very hard on her acquaintance with the wealthy bachelor.

"Islanders always come home, sooner or later," Uncle Alec asserted comfortably. "Have you found a place yet?"

"Nothing definite."

"But we're working on it," Mrs. Tarbush added swiftly, smiling up at Wellington Campbell as though she were a vital part of his team.

Aunt Janet pulled in the corners of her mouth wryly.

"I'm sure you are, Fanny," she returned, with a meaning not altogether to Mrs. Tarbush's liking.

Mrs. Tarbush steered Mr. Campbell quickly away. After all, when a woman is trying to unload a piece of property, she doesn't usually want the whole village to know she's also trying to make her hand in marriage part of the deal.

Mrs. Tarbush was not to escape the Kings so easily, however. At the door, Hetty and Olivia caught sight of Mrs. Tarbush's enormous hat approaching. Hetty, whose tongue was much sharper than Janet's, took in the dyed egret feath-ers with the bunches of artificial cherries and the many-flounced green taffeta dress beneath.

"Gad," Hetty muttered, fortunately out of the woman's hearing, "Fanny Tarbush looks like a head-on collision between a fashion plate and a nightmare!"

Chapter Nine

Soon enough, Aunt Janet, Uncle Alec, Olivia and even Hetty had forgotten all about Mrs. Tarbush. They were all sitting on the edge of their chairs in the darkened hall, utterly spellbound by Sara's performance.

The magic lantern show had sold out faster than anyone could have imagined possible. The hall was so packed that men stood up against the back wall and children sat cross-legged on the floor just in front of the stage. The combined pressure of so much expectation all came down on Sara, making her fairly tremble. She must, she had to, give her all.

So that's exactly what she did.

Sara stood at the front, on the very edge of the stage, just to the left of the sheet where the slides were being shown. And she looked quite as ethereal as she had wished to look. Indeed, all that could be seen of her was the white sweep of her dress, the crown of flowers and the gleam of her enormous eyes as she narrated the pictures before her. Jasper Dale, safely alone on the balcony, rose to the occasion too. He changed the slides, one after another, cleverly matched to the rhythms of Sara's speech. In this, his hour of glory, he seemed to have become as skilled with his hands as he was awkward with his tongue.

For maximum effect upon her audience, Sara had chosen the story of The Little Match Girl, for which Jasper just happened to have a set of slides. The tale was pathetic in the extreme, a circumstance which Sara hoped would wring great tears from the spectators and make them certain they were getting their money's worth in return for their donation.

Sara had already told the part about the little orphan match-seller, wandering the streets barefoot in the bitter cold, unable to sell a single match to heartless passers-by.

"Her poor little hands," Sara intoned, "were numb with cold. 'Oh,' she thought, 'how one little match would warm me.' She couldn't resist. She pulled one from its little box...."

Mrs. Lawson, at the old piano on the other side of the stage, was giving it her utmost, too. Her fingers beat out a long, quivering trill.

"Scr-r-atch...how it fluttered and wavered in

the night wind! It burned just like a little candle, but," Sara paused suspensefully while Mrs. Lawson struck the keys again, "what a strange light! Suddenly, the little match girl was sitting under the most amazing Christmas tree. Thousands of candles were burning on its green branches. She held out both her hands. Then, the candle started to rise higher and higher into the night air."

The slide changed, showing the girl lifting her thin, ragged arms towards the wondrous light rising before her. The piano notes rose higher and higher too, so high that Mrs. Lawson seemed in danger of running right off the end of the keyboard. Everyone in the hall leaned forward, holding their breaths.

Everyone, that is, except Sally Potts who, at the very back, said something to Jane and giggled. A whole troop of match girls could probably suffer in front of Sally and she'd never even blink.

Sara never noticed Sally. She was beyond noticing giggles, beyond noticing even the audience in the hall. One hand pressed to her heart, she felt she had drifted magically away and was in the world of the little match girl, too, surrounded by hundreds and hundreds of brilliant candles.

"One of them," she continued in a low, vibrant voice, "turned into a shooting star that streaked across the night sky. Suddenly the match went out. The light was gone. 'Someone must be dying,' she thought, for her dear, kind Granny, now long dead, had said that when a star falls, a soul goes up to Heaven."

Another slide fell into place, this time showing the emaciated child gazing up joyfully into the face of a bent old woman. Mrs. Lawson's fingers trembled across the keys, as though she were having trouble keeping them steady. The crowd was entirely mesmerized, including the whole King family. Even Aunt Hetty, no longer glowering at Sara's imaginative get-up, seemed quite melted down by the tale.

Olivia gazed at her niece proudly.

"That girl is destined for something, Hetty," she whispered, her cheeks warm with emotion.

Sara's voice rose and fell, drawing even the dullest into her narrative. The little match girl had recklessly struck the last of her matches, never thinking about what she would sell on the morrow.

"This time, in its glow, stood her old Granny, the only person who had ever been kind to her. 'Granny,' she cried, 'please don't leave me. Take me with you. Please don't leave me!'"

Deaf to the plight of the match girl, Sally and Jane slipped out the back of the main hall. Sara flung back her head so that the light from the slide made a disembodied oval of her face.

"The little match girl pleaded and pleaded with her Granny in the glow of light that surrounded them like a blanket. Granny took her dear little granddaughter in her arms..."

Sara closed her eyes, completely unaware that Sally and Jane were tiptoeing up the back stairs to peep at Jasper Dale.

"...and flew with her high, high up towards Heaven. Higher and higher they ascended, and there was no more cold or hunger or fear...."

Sally and Jane, fists against their mouths to stifle their laughter, began to creep across the balcony floor.

"But in the light of dawn, her huddled figure was found frozen to death on the first morning of the New Year. She was holding onto her matches. Nearly all were burnt down. 'She must have been trying to warm herself,' the people said, but no one knew the radiance in which she had arisen with her dear, old, kind Granny in the joy of the New Year."

Mrs. Lawson ended with a heart-stopping flourish, then let the last notes tinkle away into the silence that gripped the room. Sara stood motionless, so poised and slender in her flowing white dress that, had she but been able to float toward the ceiling, she might herself have been the beautiful spirit of the match girl ascending to heavenly bliss.

Slowly, very slowly, Sara came back to reality. Part of her was quite wrung out from the sad death of the little match girl. Another part knew that she had a theatrical triumph on her hands.

Then, the mood was broken by the sudden scraping of a chair. It was Wellington Campbell, standing up abruptly and pushing his way out along the crowded row of people. Sara glimpsed the back of his coat as he tramped out the door. Fanny Tarbush was standing up, too, gazing after him uncertainly, apparently not invited to wherever he was off to in such a hurry.

Just as dread doubt touched Sara, the crowd suddenly came to its senses. Coughs and sniffs were lost in wave after wave of applause. Hetty, determined that a King family achievement should get its full due, stood up, hauling Olivia with her. Instantly, the rest of the crowd followed suit, rising up into a standing ovation. Cries of "Bravo!" and "Well done!" echoed to the rafters, completely drowning out the clatter of Wellington Campbell's carriage driving off into the night.

Quite overcome, Sara swayed on the stage, receiving all this tribute. Her heart swelled up inside her until it felt so big she thought her chest would burst. Yes, she had done it! She had made a success of something. And even if she hadn't collected a cent for the library fund, the pleasure on the faces of the audience would have been more than reward enough.

Determined to share the glory, Sara made a sweeping motion up toward the balcony where the face of Jasper Dale was just visible. Amazingly, Jasper didn't disappear when the attention of the crowd turned to him, sending up a renewed surge of applause. In fact, Jasper bobbed his head and remained beaming down over the rail. Something like a smile shone from his flushed, bespectacled face.

My plan has worked! Sara thought joyfully. The crippling destruction of Addie McNeil was quite wiped out. Jasper was going to start trusting Avonlea folk once again!

Unfortunately, not all Avonlea folk were to be trusted. As Jasper savored his hard-won moment of honor, he failed to notice that Sally and Jane had inched across the balcony floor until they were almost at his heels. Sides shaking with mirth, they exchanged gleeful, conspiratorial glances. Under cover of the continuing applause, they sucked in one great breath.

"Three, two, one...JASPER DALE!" they exploded.

Jasper must have jumped about a foot off the floor. His feet slammed the balcony rail, his knees banged the table where the magic lantern stood, and his elbow knocked the magic lantern right over the edge of the balcony altogether. The box flew—slides, lamp and all—down, down toward the crowd below, even though Jasper himself nearly went over the rail in a sprawling, belated attempt to catch it.

Sara didn't see the magic lantern hurtling down until it crashed into the aisle halfway down the hall. Instantly, the oil lamp which had been inside it smashed open on the floor and burst into flame. One second later, the blazing kerosene had ignited the skirts of an astounded Mrs. McGee, who had the misfortune to have been standing beside it.

There is nothing like the cry of "Fire!" in a crowded hall to produce total panic and a major stampede. Instantly, before Sara's horrified eyes, pandemonium broke loose. Those near the back flung themselves at the doors and were soon streaming out as fast as their legs would carry them. Others, not caring to wait their turn at the exit, began flinging up the side windows and

tumbling out through them under the feet of a
lot of startled buggy horses. A few cooler heads
realized they had better do something about the
fire itself if Avonlea wanted to keep its Town
Hall.

Sara, farthest from the door and high up on
the stage, had a grand view of everything. Mr.
McGee leaped to the aid of his shrieking wife,
whom he helped by tearing her skirt off altogether. Her petticoat came with it, letting the whole
world see she was dressed in baggy navy
bloomers patched with mattress ticking. Half a
dozen men began to stamp madly at the flames
with their boots while others called for buckets
of water. As Mrs. McGee was hustled out, a
lanky farmer had the bright idea of grabbing
Hetty's good linen bedsheet to beat at the conflagration.

"Get out of here, girl!" he roared at Sara as he
scrambled past her to rip down the sheet.

Unable to move, Sara looked from the fire to
the balcony, where Jasper Dale was still hanging
halfway over the rail, face gaping with dismay at
the madness below.

"Mr. Dale!" Sara yelled, trying to get his attention. All she got was one wretched look before
Jasper turned around and fled as fast as he could
from the ruin of his once exultant evening.

By now, the more hardy of Avonlea's citizens were running back in with buckets, organizing themselves to deal with the emergency.

"Get out! Get out of here!" they began to shout, as if the rest of the fleeing crowd needed to be told. Someone prodded at Sara and at last she, too, set out to make her escape.

Coughing in the oily smoke that was rapidly filling the hall, Sara gave the fire a wide berth and pushed her way into the lobby. She was just in time to see Sally and Jane hanging onto one another and struggling with the rest of the people toward the outside door. Their faces were stark with something Sara instantly knew was not just fright about the fire.

Her opinion was confirmed as soon as they caught sight of her. Sally and Jane turned greenish and almost trampled old Mrs. Woodley into the floor in their attempt to get away. Sara could have sworn they had just run down the balcony stairs!

Once outside, Sara didn't have time to think, for everything was confusion. Everyone, as soon as they got in the open air, suddenly had to account for everyone else who had been inside the hall. Mothers and fathers dashed about trying to round up their children. Family groups formed and got broken up by other groups who bumped into them. Toddlers howled, the bucket brigade ran to and from the village pump and everybody else shouted at the top of their lungs.

"Sara! There you are, thank goodness. Now where on earth is Clemmie Ray?"

Sara found herself grabbed by her Aunt Janet and hustled over to the buggy where all the King children were being lined up and checked to see that they were still in one piece. Clemmie was found wandering in the street. The look on Aunt Hetty's face was indescribable.

Despite all the smoke pouring from the windows of the hall, however, the fire was soon put out. The main casualties were Hetty's bedsheet, a section of the Town Hall floor and Mrs. McGee's dignity. Mrs. McGee, wrapped in a horse blanket, was quickly carted off home by her husband.

Very soon, the crowd sorted itself out and followed after, the King family included. Sara sat gloomily in the buggy, dress smudged and her crown of flowers pulled all askew. She was beyond worrying about her appearance now. Her great success was utterly ruined, but this time it wasn't her fault at all.

Sara knew, she just knew, that what had happened inside was *not* an accident!

Chapter Ten

"Mr. Dale," Sara called out anxiously. "Mr. Dale, are you home?"

It was early the next morning after the ill-fated evening at the Town Hall. Of all the painful results of the fire the worst for Sara had been the horrible blow to Jasper Dale's newborn self-confidence. Practically all night, Sara had lain awake brooding on it. Before breakfast, even, she had run all the way over to Jasper's farmhouse and hammered on his door.

The door remained shut tight. On top of that, every curtain was drawn. No matter how much Sara rapped, no one came. After the front door, she tried the back door, then the barn, and then the front door again.

"Mr. Dale, please answer."

Her calls did no good. The house might as well have been a tomb, sealed up over the Jasper Dale who might have been, if only the Town Hall hadn't burst into flames.

With a sigh, Sara turned away. Maybe he really wasn't home, though Sara couldn't imagine where a man who had just been as humiliated as Jasper would go, except perhaps underneath his own bed. Yet she had no sooner stepped from the porch when a telltale sound brought her to a halt. It wasn't a big sound, but it was one Sara knew in an instant. It was the sound of an upstairs window closing. She dashed out into the yard—too late to see Jasper himself, but in the window right over the kitchen, the curtains were quivering.

"Mr. Dale, I know you're in there. Andrew was looking at the magic lantern and he said that it won't take much to fix it. Please come out!"

Thank goodness magic lanterns were sturdy things, and that Andrew had had the good sense to rescue this one.

No answer greeted Sara's news. The curtains were still. Sara tried again.

"I'm sorry. It wasn't your fault. Everybody knows that."

Obviously, Jasper Dale didn't know that. Nor, after the shock at the hall, Sara supposed glumly, was he likely to take her word for it. She had been the one who had enticed him there. She had been the one who had recklessly promised that everything was going to turn out fine.

With heavy steps, Sara gave up and turned for home. Her burden now was more than just loss to the library fund, it was the haunting knowledge that Jasper Dale, who had trusted her, was wounded to the marrow of his bones. Affairs weren't much better back at Rose Cottage. Hetty may have forgotten herself enough to lead a standing ovation, but she had now come back to her usual frame of mind with a vengeance. She had predicted disaster and disaster had come. And all she could think of was that the disaster would be forever linked to the name of Hetty King.

Olivia, in hopes of cheering the morning, had put on her sunniest yellow apron. She stood at the stove poaching eggs. However, if she thought the idea of a good breakfast was going to calm anyone, she was mistaken. Hetty paced up and down, too agitated even to see to the teapot.

"Don't fret so, Hetty," Olivia said placatingly, testing one of the eggs. "When all is said and done, the evening was a great success."

"A great success? Mrs. McGee goes up in smoke—you call that a great success? I shall never be able to hold my head up in public again."

Hetty was all too prone to imagining herself the prime mover behind everything that happened in Avonlea. Olivia tried to cast more oil upon the waters.

"Mrs. McGee was quite unharmed. Only her pride was hurt."

Mrs. McGee was also proof of the adage that one should always wear respectable undergarments. One never knew when there was going to be a fire and the whole neighborhood would see them.

Hetty turned her cannons in a different direction. "I knew anything involving Jasper Dale was destined for failure."

At the name, a hitch of sympathy crossed Olivia's face. She had taken a liking to Jasper, now that she had seen him up close. She hated to think what he must be feeling right now and hoped Sara was, even then, putting some things to rights.

Hetty stopped short and stared out the window past the potted geraniums to the gate.

"Oh good Lord, look who's coming over. Hide the eggs."

In astonishment, Olivia saw it was none other than Mrs. Tarbush climbing down from her buggy and heading for their door. She was clutching a handkerchief and her face was screwed up in a manner that didn't bode well for civilized conversation. Hetty opened the door a split second before the widow would have burst through it.

"Good morning, Fanny," Hetty said, pretending she didn't notice the woman's state.

Fanny Tarbush honked loudly into her handkerchief.

"There's not a good thing about it, Hetty King.

I am so upset. I hope the profit of your show has made it worth the pain it has cost me."

"Profit?" Hetty wasn't about to admit to financial gain in front of a woman she detested. "We'll be lucky to buy a dozen books after we pay for the damage."

There'd been the half dozen burnt chairs, the section of flooring that would have to be put in and Mrs. McGee's dress—not to mention the smoking ruin of Hetty's bedsheet, which broke up her most prized set. And, no doubt, Jasper Dale would want money to fix that ridiculous magic lantern contraption of his.

Fanny Tarbush sat down on a kitchen chair, treated herself to a large sob and gave her handkerchief a twist.

"What about the damage to the sale of my farm? Our deal was to close this morning," she cried, much aggrieved. What was a few dollars for a spot blaze when one had lost the benefit of a hard-won transaction in real estate.

"Well, I hardly think that's any of my affair, Fanny," Hetty said sharply. There were some things even she refused to be responsible for.

Sara came in the door from Jasper Dale's. Her face told everything about her fruitless visit. On the way back through the dewy fields, she had had time to brood upon life's unfairnesses.

Stockings soaked through, she entered the house with a slow, sepulchral tread.

"Hello, Mrs. Tarbush," she said politely. "I'm sorry to hear about Mr. Campbell."

Everyone knew that Mrs. Tarbush had had to beg a ride home last night in sour old Mr. Wade's rickety buggy. Mr. Wade raised chickens for a living and his buggy was always spotted all over from the pullets roosting on it.

"Gone!" Mrs. Tarbush lamented, twisting her handkerchief until it looked ready to scream for its life. "And after him practically asking me if my period of mourning was over."

Widows were expected to mourn for their husbands for at least a year, and to dress all in black. No gentleman could court a widow while she was still in mourning. But after the mourning was laid aside—well then, things could become very lively indeed. Mrs. Tarbush had clearly been nursing a great many hopes of Mr. Campbell in that direction.

Ignoring Mrs. Tarbush's calamity, Sara progressed funereally over to the stove.

"Do we have any hard peas, Aunt Olivia?" she asked, chin stonily set.

"Why?"

Olivia looked away from the poached eggs, very much startled.

"I wanted to put them in my shoes—for penance."

Sara's face grew even longer and paler as she contemplated her multiple tragedies. If ever there was a girl who needed to do penance, it was herself. Olivia was still looking at Sara in faint astonishment, even though she was growing familiar with Sara's dramatic turn of mind.

"I don't think Presbyterians do penance, Sara," Olivia ventured. Something very like amusement lurked at the corner of her mouth.

Denied the expiation of peas in her shoes, Sara blurted out, "It's either that, or kill Sally Potts!"

This was really what was down underneath everything—fury at Sally's low, interfering tricks.

"You'll do nothing of the kind!"

Olivia was a lot more definite about murder than she was about peas in people's shoes.

"Wellington!" groaned Mrs. Tarbush, a fat tear squeezing from each eye. "Not a word. Now this!"

Olivia kept her eye on Sara, perhaps worried about the safety of Sally Potts. Like a martyr led to execution, Sara lifted a hand to her forehead.

"I led poor Jasper Dale into untold humiliation," she lamented. "Maybe the little pebbles on the front walk will do just as well. What would you say if I went barefoot for the next week?"

"I wouldn't say anything, Sara Stanley," Aunt Hetty cried, completely out of patience at last. "I would simply put you over my knee and give you a good solid spanking. You'd find that penance enough."

Mrs. Tarbush chose this moment to abandon herself completely to yowling, luxurious sobs. Her hat quivered and her shoulders shook and her bosom heaved like a stormy sea.

"Good heavens, Olivia," Hetty whispered, "give her some eggs and send her home."

Sara wasn't allowed to put pebbles in her shoe, but she had pains enough from Avonlea's more insensitive citizens. Mrs. Ray had returned from Newbridge to discover Clemmie's defection to the magic lantern show and Edward's illicit camp-out in the woods. Both children had suffered her wrath. Edward, rubbing his sore backside, was not going to forgive Clemmie for many months to come. Clemmie had immediately run up a fever, seeming to justify her mother's darkest warnings. Mrs. Ray met Mrs. Potts at the general store. Mrs. Potts mentioned Sara Stanley. Mrs. Ray flung up her hands toward Heaven.

"Didn't I tell you she was no good? The Bible says, 'Man is born to trouble as the sparks fly upward,' and we have no better proof."

"Upward and across the room," agreed Mrs. Potts, who had been at the scene of the conflagration. "We could all have perished."

"She certainly can tell a story, though," volunteered Mr. Lawson, who had overheard them from behind the flour bins. He had enjoyed Sara's narration tremendously and wanted to defend her. The forces were two to one against him, however. Mrs. Potts immediately leaped upon his well-meant remark.

"That's exactly what she is—a Story Girl."

As though deliberately searching out a den of lions, Olivia and Sara picked this second to walk into the store. At the sight of Sara, Mrs. Ray's bony face went rigid and she bristled like a roused-up porcupine.

"Oh, hello, Miss Story Girl, I have a tale for you," she spat out acidly. "Clemmie's real sick. And it might be the measles, and the measles go awful hard with the Rays. If they don't die completely of 'em, it leaves them blind."

At this, Sara went white and her very knees turned to ice. She had been the one who had tempted Clemmie into the buggy. Of all the things she had brought upon Avonlea, the calamity that horrified her most was to be responsible for Clemmie's untimely demise.

"Has the doctor said it's measles, Mrs. Ray?"

Olivia inquired, sliding a reassuring arm round Sara's shoulder.

"Well, no, but she's feverish. Real feverish, and—" Mrs Ray gathered herself to give Sara her strongest evil eye, "—all because you played the devil with her. You've played the devil with all of us."

Mrs. Ray, at full battle pitch, was enough to frighten a small platoon. Seeing Sara quail under the assault made even the good-natured Olivia lose her temper.

"That's enough, Mrs. Ray. What kind of mother leaves her child alone overnight? Clemmie was far safer with us. I'm very sorry she's ill, but I suggest you consult a doctor before making your own diagnosis."

This outburst from someone as mild and pliant as Olivia was so surprising that even Mrs. Ray was confounded. With one opponent done in, Olivia turned to finish off the other.

"And whether she's told you or not, Mrs. Potts, it was your girl Sally who caused the fire in the first place with her mean-spirited taunting of Jasper Dale. So, before I spread the story all over Avonlea, I would suggest you take your wagging tongues elsewhere!"

Olivia finished up with a great, hot rush of breath. With her feet planted apart, she stood glowering until Mrs. Potts and Mrs. Ray picked up their purchases and decamped. Only when they were gone did Sara realize that Olivia was shaking. She gazed up at her aunt with open admiration.

"Oh, Sara!" Olivia gasped, letting her breath escape her lungs, "that felt good!"

Having tasted battle and victory in almost the the same moment, Olivia grinned at Sara with all her might. She ought to have tried losing her temper years ago.

Chapter Eleven

On the first school day after the magic lantern show, Sara arrived to find her schoolmates in a ferment about it. In fact, two factions were rapidly forming, with Sara at the hub of the controversy. A great many children confessed they had been "thrilled through" by Sara's narration. Two first-graders crowned themselves with buttercups at recess, and a couple of Sloane girls even boasted about how much they had cried when the little match girl froze to death in the snow.

Sally Potts, though, still contrived to be a cruel thorn in Sara's tender side. She and Jane were the leaders of a taunting clique which said Sara had looked like a fool in a nightgown up on the Town Hall stage. It also pointed out snidely that the school still had precious little money with which to buy books. Prominent among the anti-Sara faction was Edward Ray, who shot her a hair-raising look at the end of the day when Sara was standing in the schoolyard waiting for her cousins.

Cecily and Felicity skipped down the steps and joined Sara, scowling back at Edward. Once again, the Kings meant to stick together.

"Anyway," Cecily chimed up, "Clemmie doesn't have the measles at all. She just has a bad cold."

Sara rescued Cecily's hair-ribbon, which was about to take flight on the breeze.

"I'm so relieved, Cecily. I would never have forgiven myself if she had died of the measles."

"Ha!" snorted Felicity, who'd been snubbed cold by Mrs. Ray only that morning. "She'd probably be a whole lot happier dead than living with that horrible mother of hers."

Sally Potts, observing the united Kings from the other side of the schoolyard, decided it was time to launch a renewed attack. Followed by three other girls, Sally strolled toward Sara, skirt swaying.

"Oh look," she squeaked, in sudden, exaggerated surprise. "There's Sara Stanley, the Story Girl. Light any fires lately, match girl?"

This was too much for Felicity. Then and there, she decided she loathed Sally Potts, and she intended to take no more taunting from such a source. "You're just jealous because Sara raised more money than you did for the library fund, Sally Potts, even after she paid for the damages that *you* caused. Why don't you go home and scrub your kitchen floor and then take a mud-bath in it!"

Sally's mouth dropped open. She shut it again in a hurry.

"I don't know what you're talking about. I had nothing to do with that fire."

This lie was met with an icy glare from all the children grouped around Sara. It was the sort of moment in which battles are won or lost. An attacker must keep on attacking if she believes in her cause, or lose all credibility. Sally made the error of turning her back and walking away, trailed by her three companions. They joined Jane over by the fence and whispered contemptuously, with Sally now acting as though the matter were too ridiculous even to bother about.

Well, Sara wasn't going to let her get away with that!

"Oh yes, you did, Sally Potts," Sara shouted after them. "And I'm going to prove it if it's the last thing I do!"

Everybody heard Sara, and everybody started looking at Sally Potts. Sara was looking hotly determined, indeed.

Uneasily, Sally edged closer to Jane. "Everybody knows it's old Jasper Dale's fault."

Mentioning Jasper Dale was another mistake. Sara thought of his closed door and his mortally wounded pride. Why, he might never come outside again, even to go over to his workshop. If she did nothing else in Avonlea, she had to save him.

"You're the one that's stupid if you think you can get away with it. Confess, Sally, you're the one that started the fire."

Sally was looking a bit uneasy now, for all that she balled her hands into fists and pulled her brows down as far as they would go.

"I did not, and take your ugly face away from me. Sara the Story Girl, what a joke. Tells a tale and it goes up in smoke."

This rashly renewed offensive sent red fury climbing up Sara's insides.

"Say it," Sara shouted again. "Confess!"

Other children started to come over to see what was going on. To Sara's surprise, most of them began to gather around her and the Kings. Sally and Jane exchanged a swift look. Necks stiff, they started walking toward the gate.

"Sara the Story Girl, what a joke. Tells a tale

and it goes up in smoke," Jane flung over her shoulder, apparently unable to to think up a rhyme of her own.

Sara started after them, Felicity and Cecily at her heels. "Come on, say it!'

Sally had no intention of saying anything. Nor, seeing the forces that were assembling against her, did she intend to stick around to argue any more. She and Jane started to walk more swiftly. Once outside the schoolyard gate, they started to run.

Sara, still advancing upon them, started to run too. So did the other children. Joining into a crowd, they began chasing Sally and Jane across the field beyond the school. "Say it! Say it! Say it! Say it!" they all hollered as they went.

It was Peter, Felix and Andrew who first caught up to Sally and Jane. As luck would have it, they cornered them right on the edge of the creek where the bank was high and curving. Felix lunged for Sally.

"Got ya!" he crowed, grabbing Sally's elbow and knocking Jane down as he did so. Jane went rolling into a thick patch of burrs.

The rest of the children came galloping up, completely surrounding Sally and Jane. As usually happens when a cause has turned hopeless, there was no one left on Sally's side. Even Jane, who was scrambling to her feet, her skirt full of burrs, was looking mutinous.

Sara strode to the fore, stern and righteous. This wasn't just some childish squabble. It involved the complete reclamation of Jasper Dale.

"Confess, or we will drop you in the deep part," Sara threatened, pointing to the swirling waters below.

"Yeah, and there are giant bloodsuckers in there," Felix warned with a fearsome grimace. "I've seen them!"

Above all, Sally was terrified of bloodsuckers, perhaps because the Potts family had so little decent blood to spare. She rolled her eyes at the murky depths, having to twist because Peter was now gripping her other arm.

"Don't," she begged. Then, trying to salvage a scrap of dignity, she affected a disgusted tone. "If I confess, will these idiots let go of me?"

Sara savored the sweetness of having her enemy totally in defeat. She knew how to make the most of the moment.

"Say 'I started the fire at the Town Hall, not Jasper Dale.'"

This requirement stuck in Sally's throat so long that Felix shifted himself toward the creek. Sally's foot felt the edge of the drop.

"I caused the fire at the Town Hall, not Jasper Dale."

The words tumbled out in a grudging mumble that could scarcely be heard above the rushing of the water.

"Louder!" Sara commanded. She wished the whole of Avonlea could hear.

Felix took another step toward the creek. Now the three of them were hovering on the edge of the overhanging bank. A whirlpool of foamy water hissed underneath.

"I caused the fire at the Town Hall!" Sally yelled as loudly as she could. "Not Jasper Dale! Now, let go of me!"

Felix and Peter did just that. They released Sally so abruptly that Sally was taken completely by surprise. She had been struggling to keep away from the creek, and now she lost her balance. She teetered to one side, then the other. Then, with her arms windmilling wildly, she swayed backwards—straight into the creek below.

Her shriek would have pierced a tin washtub. Over she went, twisting and flailing, her mouth agape. She landed with an enormous splat, went completely under and came up again, wheezing and spluttering. Since the water wasn't deeper than her waist, everyone just stood where they were, hooting and laughing and not paying the least attention to Sally's renewed screams.

If Sally had been calm, she simply could have walked out of the creek. As it was, she fell down twice more before she got herself over to the edge. Grasping great handfuls of grass, she clawed her way back onto the bank and lay there coughing. Creek water streamed from every part of her. Her dress was smeared with bank mud, and rage began to fill her up like ink in a bottle. All that confessing, and she was nearly drowned anyway. In a minute, she might just pull all Sara Stanley's hair out by the roots!

"Bloodsucker on your hand!" Felix chortled, pointing. "Bloodsuckers all over you!"

Instantly, Sally forgot all about Sara Stanley. She stared down at her own knuckle where a dreadful, bloated brown blob had attached itself. And there were more brown blobs—on her elbows and her legs and her neck!

She began to scream again. Only now she was screaming and running, too. Up the bank she went, howling and slapping and leaping as though the painless creatures were eating her up alive. The last the rest of the children saw of her was her soggy dress disappearing through the birch trees, with Jane scrambling along after her as fast as she could.

Chapter Twelve

Sally's yelps brought Aunt Hetty out of the schoolhouse, just too late to see the worst of the dunking. But she did spot Sara at the head of the crowd of children, and long experience informed Aunt Hetty that Sara had just become a real leader among the Avonlea youth.

"Sara Stanley," Aunt Hetty called out. "You come here this minute."

Oh oh! Sara thought.

She felt ready to endure any amount of trouble, though, in return for the confession that had just been extracted from Sally Potts. The confession had had all the satisfaction of divine retribution.

Sara turned—and was greeted by the unusual sight of Wellington Campbell standing beside her aunt in the schoolyard. As decorously as she could, Sara walked back. She tried hard not look as though she had just been throwing insufferable girls into creeks.

"How do you do, Mr. Campbell," she said, as the man gravely shook hands with her.

Sara followed her aunt and Mr. Campbell inside the school, and when Mr. Campbell dared to perch himself sideways on the edge of Aunt Hetty's hallowed desk, Aunt Hetty didn't say a word, Sara braced herself as Mr. Campbell addressed her.

"The last time we met, Sara Stanley, you were at the point of asking me for a fairly sizable donation to a certain library fund."

So that was it! Sara gritted her teeth. She had tried to bury forever the fiasco at the White Sands Hotel, but she could see that Mr. Campbell meant to resurrect the memory.

"Yes, Mr. Campbell?"

Sara braced herself more stoutly. Mr. Campbell pulled on his mustache a moment, as though planning how to approach the subject.

"But you see, young lady, I hate to part with my money unless I receive some benefit from the expenditure. Now as for your performance..."

Sara swallowed, remembering that the first thing she had heard after ending her performance was the sound of Mr. Campbell making for the door.

"I'm sorry you didn't enjoy the show, Mr. Campbell," Sara cut in hastily, anxious to avoid unflattering comments about her narration. "I'll give you your money back if you like."

All this grand gesture did was to amuse Mr. Campbell. One side of his mustache twitched.

"What makes you think I didn't enjoy it?"

"You left before the applause."

And left in a hurry, too, as though he had been waiting for the first possible moment to make his escape.

"Sara...I may call you Sara, may I?"

The request was very polite. The important Mr. Campbell seemed to be softening up right before Sara's eyes.

"Please do," Sara invited, a little relieved. "I prefer it to Story Girl, which is what everyone is calling me now."

"And a most appropriate name it is, for that's what you are, Sara Stanley, and never be ashamed of it."

Mr. Campbell showed open pleasure. Obviously, Sara thought, he had had no experience with Mrs. Ray.

"Your performance the other night," he went on, "seemed to move the audience in a way I've rarely seen."

Breath hitched in Sara's throat. When Sara had got up the nerve to speak in front of all those people, this was what she had been wanting passionately to achieve. She hoped she had done it. She felt she had done it. But to hear Mr. Campbell say it aloud here in the schoolroom seemed suddenly to make it all quite true.

A radiant look stole across Sara's face. She seemed to be having this conversation privately, as if Aunt Hetty weren't even there at all. "My mother used to read me that story," Sara confided, distant, cherished memories welling up.

"Your mother must have been very proud watching you."

Sara clasped her hands in front of her. Her voice fell away to a whisper.

"She passed away when I was little."

This caught Mr. Campbell by surprise. He fell silent for a long moment, then smiled sadly in fellow feeling.

"My mother passed away when I was little, too. The way you told that story, it reminded me of her."

Right then, it dawned on Sara that people never forgot their mother, no matter how grown-up they got—even as grown-up as Mr. Campbell. And to think, she had imagined him impatient with the match girl!

"So that's why you left early," Sara breathed. "Sometimes it's a pity that your face can't show what your heart is feeling. But I suppose that's how it is for men of your stature. It would be like seeing the King of England in tears."

Mr. Campbell made a choking sound, very much as if he were smothering a laugh.

"Well, hardly the King of England!"

"Just the same," Sara went on, thinking of the awful dangers a man such as Mr. Campbell exposed himself to if he wore his feelings on his sleeve, and how hard it must be to go on being polite. "My Aunt Janet says that Fanny Tarbush would talk the ear off a pig if she had half a chance."

Mr. Campbell tugged at his mustache to keep from laughing some more, and even Hetty smiled behind her hand. More soberly, Mr. Campbell extracted a piece of paper from his pocket and handed it, with some ceremony, to Sara.

"Sara, I want you to have this as my donation to the library fund." The paper looked just like any ordinary piece of paper. But when Sara got a good look at it, she gasped, and continued gasping until Mr. Campbell laid a kind hand on her shoulder.

"A thousand dollars? Mr. Campbell, this would build a whole new library, let alone fill one with books."

Sara supposed that Mr. Campbell had made some sort of stupendous check-writing mistake. However, he seemed to know very well what was on the slip he had handed her. He only nodded, as though building new libraries was something he did whenever he fancied some light recreation.

"That's right, but you never get something for nothing in this life. I only ask that the library be named in honor of my mother."

"And so it shall, Mr. Campbell," Aunt Hetty assured him staunchly. "And we are most grateful, all of us."

From her tone, Sara guessed that Aunt Hetty would never say another disparaging word about magic lantern shows as long as she lived.

The moment Sara had said a heartfelt goodbye to her benefactor and got outside the school again, she set out as fast as her legs could carry her down the road and across the fields to Jasper Dale's farm. Oak trees and fenceposts and nodding asters fairly shot by in her hurry to get there. She was singing inside, dancing, flying. She didn't care how determinedly Jasper Dale had locked himself up in his house. Sara meant to get him out!

Jasper couldn't have known she was coming, but he had ventured out all on his own. Sara spotted his lanky form at the top of the pasture behind the barn. He was bent over his camera, exactly the way he had been when she had first met him. The black cloth was draped over his head and he appeared to be trying to get a bank of daisies into focus.

"Mr. Dale, Mr. Dale," Sara shouted, tearing through the gate and up the grassy slope. "I have to talk to you about what happened. Sally Potts confessed in front of the whole school. Now the whole town will know she caused the fire, and that's not all. Mr. Campbell made a huge donation toward the school library fund, just because he loved the show."

Unable to contain herself, Sara found that the words all came spilling out before she had even stopped running. She bent over, madly trying to catch her breath. Jasper Dale had jerked himself out from under the camera cloth and now stood like a very tall stork, staring at her through his spectacles. When Sara straightened, she told him about the thousand-dollar check all over again. Then she tried to look as dignified as she could, for what she had to say next was very important.

"I want you to know," she told Jasper sincerely, "that we couldn't have done it without you, Mr. Dale. Thank you for not letting me down."

Sara's words seemed to go through Jasper like a wind shaking a tree. The gratitude shining from her eyes made him turn first a warm pink, then a fiery red. He hitched from one boot to the other and back again. His eyebrows quivered and his shoulders jumped. Last of all, his mouth worked—and finally produced a gigantic smile.

At once, Sara let go a great whoosh of relief. He was standing taller already. He could stride into Avonlea still gathering the glory of the magic lantern show and knowing that no one blamed him for the fire. She hadn't been wrong in luring him out of hiding after all.

"Funny how things go, isn't it?" she mused. "I was beginning to think that what Aunt Hetty said was right. You know, about what was doomed to failure once is doomed to failure twice, but I think things can sometimes turn out better the second time, don't you agree?"

Apparently, Jasper Dale did. His head bobbed again. His nice brown eyes blinked happily. Even his Adam's apple got into the act.

"You are un-un-unstoppable, Sara Stanley!" he got out in one enthusiastic rush.

Jasper tried to shake hands, but found that one hand was holding his camera cloth and the other was balancing the tripod.

"N-now you know why they call me the Awkward Man," Jasper chuckled.

Jasper Dale was actually making a joke about himself! A joke that said the nickname didn't hurt him so much any more.

Clumsily, he managed to shift things around until he got one of his hands free. With it, he clasped Sara's hand and shook it heartily. Sara broke into a sunny grin. "Well, we've both got a name, then, because they're starting to call me the Story Girl. And you know, the way things have turned out, I don't think I mind one bit!"

She never did mind, either. She grew very proud of the name, for it had won her and Jasper Dale the respect and affection of Avonlea.